**DEDICATED TO ALL
MY CAMP FRIENDS**

# GENESIS

# PART I

Rabbi Nachman of Breslov is famous for saying, "The whole world is a very narrow bridge, and the most important thing is not to be afraid." The summer between high school and college is yet another bridge, narrower still, spanning the gap between who you were and who you will become.

There are two most important things about this narrower bridge. You only have to cross once, and you only get to cross once.

In 1986, after five years as a camper, I became a *machon*, a junior counselor at the Paley Lithwick Summer Institute. Joining staff ushered me into rituals that had developed over the camp's twenty-five-year history. Of these, the most important was the bar mitzvah, so called because it took place in a bar. After the campers went to sleep, a skeleton crew of counselors remained behind to keep an eye out, while most of us piled into cars bound for the Stockyard, a pool hall with low ceilings, hummingbird wallpaper, two well-loved video game consoles, and a foosball with half the men beheaded or broken in some way.

Jason Harris, son of camp director Mick Harris and senior counselor in the other boys cabin in my unit, officiated Steve Raben's bar mitzvah. "Friends, Hebrews, Countrymen," he began, brandishing the requisite pool cue and triangle rack. "We are gathered to celebrate the coming of age of our distinguished, learned, and, dare I say, movie-star-handsome friend?" We clapped and hooted. "A big mazel tov to Steve ben Melvin v'Eileen, proud Mosquito Scout and junior assistant vice president of the storied lost tribe of Anheuser-Busch."

With his feathered hair and muscled thighs, Jason came across more like a cheerleader than a master of ceremonies. "Young Steve may still be laboring under the false impression that his bar mitzvah was observed at the age of thirteen, but let us permanently and decisively eradicate that misbegotten fable. Steve, *boychick*, please approach the *bima* so that I can administer the first of the ten commandments of this ancient and beloved rite of passage."

Shoved forward by his friends, Steve took his place by Jason's side with a sheepish yet stoic wave. Trina Abrams and I leaned against the foosball table. I hissed into her ear that we didn't have to stay.

"Where else would we go?"

"Ever been to Yon Yonson's?"

"I hear it's nasty, and besides, I want to see this."

"Like it's not nasty here?"

"*Sha!*" she snapped. "You're supposed to be Steve's friend."

Assisted by two other counselors, Jason lifted the bar mitzvah boy to his place of honor on the countertop. He spoke into the pool cue. "Now Steve, since I'm feeling generous tonight, I will allow you to select the first commandment." Steve leaned into the pool cue and requested a Jägermeister, raising an appreciative murmur.

"Barbaric," I said.

"Jealous," she accused.

"Every year, somebody ends up in the emergency room."

"Yeah, but not Steve. He's the man of steel," Trina replied, as if this were a salacious nugget.

After downing his shot, the bar mitzvah boy was commanded to consume nine more items from the Stockyard menu—not all of them alcoholic. He gnawed an oversize cocktail olive stuffed with bleu cheese. He took a long drag from a filter-tip Kool menthol 100 and blew a passable ring. I was called upon to microwave the *boychik* a mug of Swiss Miss with dehydrated marshmallows. When I returned to Trina's side, she gave my ass a friendly squeeze.

Truth be told, I still carried a torch for, among others, Cheryl Gilman, another *machon,* who'd let me get to not-quite-third base on the last night of camp the previous summer. On the last night, things happened that wouldn't normally happen. Things went a little further. I didn't know it yet, but there would be no last night of camp for me this summer.

Cheryl hadn't taken kindly to my suggestion that we pick up in 1986 where we had left off in 1985, but there were moments when our eyes met and a current seemed to pass between us, though I invariably looked away too quickly. This was just one of numerous crushes that weighed on me. "Crush" was the wrong word. Each girl was a syndrome with her own distinct set of symptoms. They occupied a double album's worth of half-written songs, spread across four notebooks and as many years of high school.

I would never write a song for Trina. The more interest she showed in me, the less I reciprocated. She had an air of experience that I both recoiled from and hoped would infect me. And a car! She was also very good with the campers, instinctively knowing when to treat them like a friend and when to administer discipline.

It was no accident that Rochelle Strauss, the only daughter of philanthropist Franklin Strauss, had been assigned to Trina's cabin. There were no ostentatious privileges bestowed upon the girl—she ate the same food and slept on the same mattress as the rest of us—but she enjoyed an ineffable deference up and down the camp hierarchy.

She addressed campers, counselors, and rabbis alike in the same amiable tone that in another era would have been used on servants, but with enough of a wink under the noblesse oblige that we felt appreciated. We were in awe of her. Not just me, all of us, hypnotized by the iridescent flecks dancing along her cheekbones, suggestive of internal heat.

The bar mitzvah service rolled along, with Steve chasing a slice of pepperoni pizza with a frosty mug of St. Pauli Girl and a cup of Lipton alphabet soup that had been doctored to contain only a P, a U, two S's and a Y. At other religious camps, did similar rituals take place, with the Stations of the Cross or the Analects of Confucius invoked instead of the Ten Commandments? The combination of ingredients interacting in Steve's system reddened his face and stung his eyes. After the slurping of an overflowing 7&7, all that remained of his rite was a foil-wrapped vending machine kielbasa, which he sportingly covered with ketchup, mustard, and a heaping spoonful of Kryptonite-green relish before scarfing.

"By the way," I said, "I know what song we should sing for the Talent Show."

"Are you going to sing with me?" Trina perked up.

"You and I are going to harmonize their socks off. Me James, you Carly."

"'You're So Vain'?"

"No, that's the song she sang *about* him after the breakup. The song they sing together is 'Mockingbird'."

When the last of the kielbasa had been choked down, Jason ceremoniously placed the triangle rack over Steve's beet-colored, sweat-soaked head and pointed right at me, declaring that the next night out would bring my turn to become bar mitzvah. *Hava N'gila* erupted, with us all swinging each other about the bar and dancing with the honoree in a chair raised high above our heads. The wallpaper hummingbirds wheeled around us. Did the frenzy mock or honor our Ashkenazi ancestors? If pressed, none of us would quite have been able to say which.

While Jason walked Steve around the Stockyard parking lot, five of us climbed into Trina's yellow Gremlin and returned to camp. Leaning forward from the middle of the back seat, I ejected Squeeze's *Singles—45s and Under* and inserted Paul Simon's latest into the tape deck. The music played loud enough to be heard over the balmy air rushing into the windows.

*These are the days of miracle and wonder*
*This is the long distance call*
*The way the camera follows us in slo-mo*
*The way we look to us all, oh yeah.*

When Trina offered to walk me back to my cabin, I said it was late.

"A little walk with me will help you sleep."

"Actually," I said, "It would rob me of sleep."

"I'll make it worth the tired, Eric."

I gave her a peck on the cheek and slipped away, though not in the direction of my cabin.

Did the summer of 1986 teach me anything at all? Not right away, but over time it has become clear that there's no such thing as doing right for the wrong reason. And that being young means you can fail spectacularly and suffer no consequences. And that beautiful girls can disappear twice without ever being gone.

# PART II

Before I knew it I was standing over her.

Rochelle's legs were long and strong, but the skin was a disaster. A thicket of sun-white down coated her lap, with its blurry tan bisecting a few old bruises that had faded to a mottled yellow. One of her dirty kneecaps shone with a picked scab. A dozen or so short dark hairs that had been missed by the razor, more than once, curled from each shin, their follicles inflamed. Four or five fading friendship anklets separated a relatively healthy brown from fish-belly-white feet dangling lavender flip-flops. Just a few flecks of dark wine lacquer remained on the toenails.

She sprawled on the stoop of a cabin, not her own, a paperback cast aside, and didn't speak when I took a seat beside her. Not a single mosquito in the State of Wisconsin had been able to resist the taste of Rochelle's legs. In a few days, when the designation of "the last one to see Rochelle alive" would temporarily and then ironically attach to me, I would mentally scour those limbs like a man desperate to find his way out of the wilderness with only a mangled map.

Rochelle's face, in contrast, was as perfect as a glass of milk, a porcelain cloud framed by granite-black ringlets. Clear eyes with dappled cobalt irises threatened to suck me into their vortices, just as they had four days earlier, when we were clinging to a red kayak in the middle of a sudden storm on Lac du Bois. I wasn't ready to think about that.

"Birthday buddy!" I grinned, picking up the book. *Zen and the Art of Motorcycle Maintenance*—disappointing as literature but inspired as accessory. Could the color of her flip-flops have been selected intentionally to match the puce-purple of the book's cover?

"How was Steve R's bar mitzvah?"

"Didn't Trina catch you out here last night? You're not supposed to know about the whole bar mitzvah thing. When I was a camper I had no idea."

"You went to camp here?"

A dramatic imbalance—between what I knew about her life and what she knew about mine—warped the space between us. Rochelle dwarfed me, even though I had a good six inches on her. Her whisper drowned out my scream. (That was a good one; it definitely belonged in my notebook of song lyrics.) She was rich, but more than that, she was famous, without celebrity but rather a humming, crackling aura. We all wanted her to sign her name on our possessions, on our skin if necessary. We wanted to snap her picture. By contrast, when people addressed me without using my name, I always suspected they'd forgotten it.

"Did Trina tell you she found me here? And besides, it smells like Anne Frank's period in my cabin. You wouldn't make me go back there, would you, birthday buddy?" One brow lifted slightly, shifting the way the light hit her cheekbone.

"I so love this book," I heard myself marvel. "What he says about changing the world by changing your life—it changed my life. 'The place to improve the world is first in one's own heart and head and hands, and then work outward from there.'"

"Exactly!"

"We're just friends," I added.

"Who?"

"Trina and me."

"Too bad for Trina."

"I guess," I said.

"I liked your—" she started to say, and I hoped the sentence would finish with "song," but it was drowned out by the sputter of a scooter motor.

I was no athlete. I would never get ahead in business with or without trying, but original songs held untold promise. Jewish boys just like me had made themselves legendary singer-songwriters. Bob Dylan, Paul Simon, and Leonard Cohen were my Holy Trinity. Dylan was the Father, merciless and omniscient, sending blues chords down like thunderbolts on his idolatrous flock. Paul Simon walked the earth as God's flawed human embodiment, the voice of wonder and anguish, wisdom and wounded pride. "I Am a Rock" and "American Tune" blew me away, but at least I could imagine writing them. Aloof and removed, Leonard Cohen altogether surpassed my teenage understanding. Dylan and Simon both had praised him, so I knew he was the genuine article, but his songs demanded adult experience. Suzanne, Marianne, Bernadette betokened flavors my tongue couldn't taste yet.

The sentence she had begun mattered a little too much. Did she really like "Shrinking World," the song about childhood that I'd written for services? Black-mustached, black-leather-clad Rabbi Mick dismounted the red Vespa and approached. "It's after ten. What are you two—"

"Asthma attack," Rochelle said, producing a corn-colored inhaler as evidence.

"Hop on," Mick bellowed, a command both tender and reproachful, coming just a few days after she had trespassed upon the sanctity of his personal vehicle. She'd hopped on and looped once around the soccer field, her black ringlets dancing as we all watched gape-mouthed. A volcano of rage had seemed to be on the brink of eruption before his inner fundraiser had whispered to him that some campers were permitted infractions that would be otherwise be most severely punishable.

I'd witnessed her larceny, gawked at the circling figure enveloped by a force field comprising not just attractiveness and wealth but another intangible, untouchable, inborn majesty.

"I'll take you to the nurse," Mick reiterated. "Weintraub, back to your cabin, now."

"I'm fine," she smiled. "See you both in the morning. Thanks, Eric. I really liked the song you played at services tonight, "Sinking World.""

Mick and I watched her flip-flop away on those gorgeous ruined legs, Mick's leather creaking as he rocked from boot to boot. He didn't have a toothpick in his mouth, but he mumbled as if he did. "Think they're gonna Rat Fuck tonight?"

"Probably," I answered, the emphasis on the last syllable. "It is Thursday."

"They Rat Fuck," he drawled, ruminating on the imaginary toothpick, "they pay."

"I remember when I was a camper, us and the other boys cabin just kept Rat Fucking back and forth for what must have been like a full hour. It was like the counselors decided that all the fun would go out of it if they just left us alone. And they were kind of—" Just then the off-key yawp of a dozen adolescent males reverberated against the empty sky.

RAT FUCK!

Rabbi Mick stomped over to his scooter.

CHICKEN SHIT! came the obligatory response from the adjacent cabin. Mick sped down the hill toward the horseshoe-shaped configuration of boys cabins known as the Horseshoe. I picked the inhaler up and put the mouthpiece to my lips, even though it probably had never touched Rochelle's.

Here's what was going on inside those cabins. Two of the boys were begging the others to stop, for god's sake, before Rabbi Mick came. Five or more were lobbying suggestions for the next volley.

"Hairy vagina, hairy vagina."

Oliver Berkowitz's head bobbed with intensity that his forefathers had reserved for the lord's unspeakable name. "Snake semen. No! Salmon semen! Salmonsemen salmonsemen salmonsemen..."

"Let's do Mick's tits." And a consensus quickly built before someone counted 3, 2, 1.

MICK'S TITS!

The rabbi skidded into the Horseshoe and killed the motor. Teenage-boy banter ceased as he stalked into the cabin, halogen flashlight blazing. His footsteps echoed as he walked three times back and forth between the rows of bunk beds. Before he said a word, Oliver asserted, "I didn't shout anything."

"You totally shouted 'Rat Fuck' louder than anyone," answered a voice in the bunk below him.

The boys fell silent as Mick cleared his throat and paced some more. He switched off his flashlight like a cowboy crushing a cigarette. "We're going to do this the most democratic way possible. We're going to take a vote. Majority rules."

"But I didn't shout anything."

"You don't get a vote, Oliver. You also don't get to talk. Not. Another. Word. The rest of you get to vote on the matter I'm putting before you, and I want you to carefully consider the consequences of your decision."

"Option A., Every single one of you forfeits mail and canteen for the rest of the session. No letters, no packages, no Snickers, no blue Mr. Freezes. Nothing.

"Option B., Oliver Berkowitz is sent home. I call his parents tonight and they pick him up in the morning."

Oliver tried to stifle his sobs as a bloodthirsty chatter went through the cabin. Rabbi Mick silenced them and asked for a show of hands, first for Option A, then for Option B. Oliver's swollen face glimmered with tears and snot, and convulsions shook his small frame.

"DOUBLE DILDO!" came a wail from the adjacent cabin, followed by a lengthy embarrassed hush.

There was nowhere in the world that Oliver Berkowitz would rather be than this poorly appointed reform Jewish summer camp in the middle of a Wisconsin swamp, with twice-daily religious services and daily study on Zionist themes, on top of Hebrew instruction, prayers before and after meals, and song sessions after meals. Even though Oliver didn't believe in the God of Moses (he identified as Zoroastrian), hated mosquitoes and Hebrew and, especially, Hebrew songs, he deeply dreaded exile to his comfortable home in Glencoe, a Swedish foreign exchange student named Lina, his school friends, a job in the downtown Glencoe ice cream parlor. Camp was the only place he felt like himself.

In full Clint Eastwood mode, Mick took his time gathering votes. Indecipherable rasps were heard as he made his way from bed to bed. By a slim margin, Oliver was permitted to remain at camp for the rest of the session. His cabin mates mercifully granted him the privilege of more mediocre institutional food, more rounds of *Hinei Ma Tov*, more Rat Fucks and skits about Theodor Herzl. The boy went fetal, and Rabbi Mick got back on his Vespa and puttered away.

"Is it my fault he has tits?" Oliver wondered aloud. "His gynecomastia is a tragedy, but don't blame me."

# PART III

My first actual conversation with Mick had occurred in April when I interviewed for the *machon* position. He kept an office in the basement of an orthodox *shul* in Skokie. The bracketed shelves were empty, the walls bare except for a black leather motorcycle jumpsuit hanging on a peg. The seat of his chair was a good four inches higher than that of the chair across the desk.

Mick stared down at me like a vulture contemplating the remains of another vulture's lunch. I reached for a prayer book on his desk, ran my fingers along the built-in red satin bookmark, and then replaced it. "I got one of these for my bar mitzvah," I ventured. "The chairwoman of the temple sisterhood presented it to me at the service, but it was kind of awkward because she called me Derek instead of Eric. And then when I looked inside, it actually said Derek Feinberg on the bookplate. Instead of Eric Weintraub."

Mick had no response to this favorite anecdote of mine. He told me the history of the camp. How it had been named Paley Lithwick for the two founding benefactors—pioneers in the Reform movement and co-authors of an influential study on Jewish education—and stayed that way for a quarter-century. Just six months earlier, it had become Paley Lithwick Strauss, having received a bequest in the amount of $300,000 from Frank Strauss, who had never visited the camp and had met Mick only once, fleetingly, at a Bulls game.

"He asked if we had an indoor swimming pool. I told him we had a lake," Mick recalled. "And he asked if I believed God had created the world in seven days. I said, 'Look at number twenty-three down there. It must have taken at least twice that'."

Rabbi Mick had never been ordained as a rabbi, but somehow the title fit. "Why do you want to be a *machon*, Eric?"

"I, um, really really like camp. I've learned so much there. Guitar, espe-cially. Maybe I could even be a song leader sometimes, when the regular one is out, or maybe at services or something.

"But not just guitar!

"My best friends are there. Tony and the Steves and Trina and, oh yeah, Jason, of course." He said nothing, so I continued, "It's not like it's perfect or anything. I know that. The cabins are kind of run down, and Noah's Ark is an out-and-out biohazard. The 'sand' at Lac du Bois is mostly these really sharp stones that cut your feet to shit, sorry, and the water is really really cold. I mean, I know you can't do anything about the temperature of the water."

"Unless we got that pool," he said, mercifully cutting me off.

"What does Frank Strauss do?" I asked. "I mean, how does he make the money to give to camp?"

"He buys companies that are about to go out of business."

"But that sounds like a way to *lose* money."

"Even when he loses money, he makes money. That's how rich he is." I nodded. It was a relief that he wasn't asking me about my family or, specif-ically, my parents' separation, which still hadn't been explained to me suffi-ciently. My father had made the decision to leave, and it had surprised my mother, but no further details were forthcoming. Financially, things must not have been great, because my mother had sold the house in a hurry and moved us from a Northbrook mini-mansion to a Morton Grove bungalow.

"A few things about becoming staff, Eric. It's a whole new world for you. The camp is the same, but last year you stood on one side of a bright line, and this year you'll be standing on the other. Can you handle that?" I nodded. "As staff, we are there to coach, to mentor, to teach these young people. Don't think you're there to hand down punishment. We don't *do* punishment at Paley Lithwick Strauss. We don't insult, humiliate, or confis-cate. We don't keep mail away from the campers. That's actually a federal offense, understand?" I said I did.

"Let me give you a hypothetical. Do you know what that means?" I said I did. "Let's say you and your cabin are walking to the lake for a swim. You're halfway there when you realize you left behind one camper, let's call him Ira. The boys know the way to the lake, so you send them ahead and return to the cabin. When you get there, you find Ira on his bed, completely naked, left hand flying up and back." He waited for my nod of comprehension. "What do you say?"

"I don't say anything. What could I say?"

"Your eyes meet. A pink plastic pump of Jergen's clatters to the floor. His hairless torso glistens in the slanted afternoon sunrays. You can't not say something, can you?"

"No, I guess not. I would tell him it's okay. 'It's okay to explore your body. Your body is changing and surging with hormones at this age. You're not doing anything wrong. You're not a bad person.' That's what I would say." Rabbi Mick made no reply, so I asked, "Why, what *should* I say?"

"You should say, 'Ira, hurry up or you'll be late for swimming'."

# PART IV

Twenty steps from the cabin stood the boys' bathroom, a cinderblock bunker called Noah's Ark after a faded Biblical mural on the outside. Several years earlier, a clever child had endowed one of the two zebras with a set of extra-large black genitalia. Maintenance had successfully bleached off the Magic Marker, leaving the beast with a blurry but discernible set of white genitalia. Predictable diagrams, limericks, and boasts covered the interior walls, courtesy of generations of adolescent boys.

*Missing: one foreskin. Generous reward if found!*

*Warning: Blow Dryers are NOT for Blow Jobs."*

Doron Ba'al Shem Tov turned to me the morning after the Rat Fuck, as we brushed our teeth in adjacent sinks. "You want to fuck her?"

"Huh?"

"Rochelle!"

"Maybe," I said. "Let me get back to you."

"What about Tammy? She's a slot, right?"

"I think you mean slut."

"So you agree with me. Anybody can see that, right?"

"Actually," I said, "Now that I think about it, *slot* is much more offensive than *slut*." We both wore nothing but towels wrapped around our waists, our chests exposed—mine pale and concave and his bronze and paunchy. Whenever Doron smiled, he looked like he was getting ready to spit blood and teeth. It was a mangled grimace, with one incisor gone and one canine recently capped in gold. His black eyes twinkled with tears never shed. Reportedly, back in Jerusalem he had impregnated a Hasidic girl, and his family had shipped him to southern Wisconsin until tempers cooled.

He had little interest in teaching Hebrew, coaching soccer, or leading discussions on religious topics, less still in telling suburban American going-into-tenth-graders what to do. When not spewing obscenities in heavily accented English, he flirted with the girl campers and took long naps.

"Then she *is* a slot," he grinned, his mouth foaming at the corners. "Am I pronouncing it right? Rhymes with twat?"

"You're not related to Yehuda Amichai, are you?" I asked.

"This is a fresh idea to you? Don't pretend, it's just us in here. If you had permission to fuck one of them, Rochelle or Tammy, which one would it be?" He put the question to me as though it was one that rabbis had been debating for centuries, as though the quality of my reply would determine my quality as a man. "Two bedrooms, two beds, two girls. Behind door number one, Rochelle. Behind door number two, Tammy. Let's make a deal!"

"They're *campers*," I protested.

"Yeah," agreed Doron. "Did you ever notice Tammy's nipples after swimming? She practically narped my eyes out yesterday. Then again, I wish it was me that found Rochelle last night. 'Oh, Eric, I can't sleep, my throat hurts'." His voice climbed up an octave and acquired a reasonably flat Midwestern accent. "'I need something hard to suck on. Do you have anything hard I can suck on, Eric? By the way, I *really* liked your song about kittens."

I gargled and spat. "That's why some of us call her *Blow-chelle*, my friend."

Doron suddenly thrust his bronze face all the way up to mine. Our noses were almost touching. In this contest, at least, I outmatched him. Above the capillary-cracked whites of his eyes, caterpillar brows popped up and down. "Are you fucking serious?" he asked, before letting a gob of toothpaste foam dribble down his chin. "That's it. I swear, if Tammy even touches me tonight, if she so much as exhales within arm's reach, if our eyes even meet once, I'm going to drag her into a *kita* and insert a few shekels into her slot."

Suddenly we realized we weren't alone. Oliver Berkowitz's round face loomed in the mirror. Doron and I exchanged glances.

"Those are my friends," Oliver said. He wore briefs and a My Eyes Are Up Here T-shirt. The knees of his spindly, hairless legs were touching.

"We weren't saying anything," Doron spat. "I don't know what you think you heard."

"I know what I heard," the boy answered. "And I know exactly who I'm going to tell about it. Tammy Hamelin's mom has ovarian cancer. Her dad might just be almost as big an asshole as you are, and she's having a hard enough time as it is. And we all know who Rochelle Strauss is. Do you think her father would find this conversation amusing?" His large forehead glowed with indignation. "Eric, you owe her better than this."

"Oliver," I pleaded. "You have to understand about Noah's Ark. It's what lawyers call a free-speech zone. Look around you, read the writing on the walls. This is a space where unsafe thoughts can be safely expressed."

"He's right, Oliver," Doron said. "Don't trample our freedom of expression."

The boy didn't blink. "This isn't Israel," he said. "What you did is a serious crime in this country."

"What crime?" Doron scowled.

"Maybe in the Promised Land you can molest young girls and get away with it," Oliver accused. "As long as it's not Shabbat. But here we call it statutory rape."

Doron zipped his I.D.F.-issue toiletry kit and started to walk away, muttering, "I'm getting out of here. Something smells like a yeast infection."

Oliver blocked the counselor's way. "We all know about the Hasidic girl. The girls are scared of you. They think you're a predator."

I urged them both not to make a thing out of this. Peacemaking fell naturally upon me, as I could relate to each of them better than they could relate to each other. Doron and I were both staff. Oliver and I were both Americans and decent human beings. I reminded them we had to get to breakfast, but they ignored me, standing toe to toe in sandaled feet.

"I know everything," Oliver sneered.

"Look at Sherlock in his girly underpants," Doron shot back. "What do you know, Sherlock?"

"I know about the underage Hasidic girl you got pregnant. I know you're about that close to being extradited."

Doron let his towel and kit drop and took a step closer. "First of all, the girl isn't Hasidic, she's orthodox, there's a difference. Second of all, she had a miscarriage." He wrapped his strong brown arms around the boy in a cold, fleshy embrace. "And do you know why she miscarried?" he hissed. "She swallowed a bottle of sleeping pills because a little pussy like you had to go and tell everybody what happened. Does that make you feel brave, you little pussy shit? You little pussy shit baby killer?" Oliver doubled over, struggling to break Doron's grip and coughing out something yellow and stringy.

"C'mon, Oliver," Doron said, letting the boy drop to the putrid cement floor. "You don't want to miss *hamotzi* before breakfast."

I followed Doron back into the cabin and asked if any of that was true. He was still naked.

"Not a single fucking word," he cackled.

# EXODUS

# PART I

Campers skipped breakfast all the time. There were always morning swims across the lake, breakfast horseback rides, special study sessions with Rabbi Y'raeh, and other excuses real and faked. I didn't notice Rochelle's absence until Trina sidled up and hurriedly whispered that the campers had been told she was in the infirmary, recovering from an asthma attack. Rabbi Mick was off campus, presumably dealing with the situation while his son Jason did his best to maintain normalcy.

She put a cool hand on my neck. "And listen, I'm also supposed to ask everyone if they've seen Mick's scooter."

"Not since last night. Why, does this have something to do with…"

"Possibly, I don't know," she said. "I have to go, but let's talk later. You're under a lot of pressure, and I want to be—"

"*Sheket B'vakasha!*" It was the irrefutable call for silence. Jason Harris stood taller and more erect than his father, but he suffered from a severe lack of gravitas. When he stood before the campers after the meal, his pep had an oddly dispiriting effect.

"*Boker tov,*" he smiled. "I've got a few announcements to make."

A few attentive campers seized on the word. "Announcements?…" they repeated, setting off a tedious ritual.

> *Announcements, announcements, annou-wou-ouncements*
> *A horrible way to die, a horrible way to die*
> *A horrible way to start the day, a horrible way to die.*

Jason had no choice now but to play his part. He held up his clipboard and exaggeratedly recited, "Directly after breakfast, we…"

*Ja-son, Ja-son, shake your bushy tail.*

Jason turned around and waggled his butt.

*Ja-son, Ja-son, shake your bushy tail.*
*Crinkle up your little nose,*
*Hold your nuts between your toes,*
*Ja-son, Ja-son, shake your bushy tail.*

All across the country, rituals that cemented the faith to seemingly ir-reverent whimsy unfolded at summer camps run by Mormons, Muslims, and Methodists. They made indoctrination fun. Jason made the prescribed effort to fold one leg so that the toe of his sneaker touched his own crotch. Smiling broadly, he held up the clipboard and theatrically repeated the first announce-ment, only to be drowned out by:

*You're in trouble, Jason!*
*You're in trouble, Jason!*
*Jason has urine trouble!*

He made a *tsk, tsk* motion with his fingers and endured the remainder of the standard announcements torment. We were released back to our cab-ins for *nikayon* and to put on our *beged-yam* because we'd be moving directly to swimming from *ivrit* without another chance to change, but first Jason made an oblique reference to the Rochelle situation. "Counselors, please re-port directly to me any mention at all regarding the topic of today's routine curricular session."

✡

For a while after college, Jason made promotional videos for an inter-national hotel chain. A sex tape scandal involving the underage niece of a European monarch made him a tangential tabloid figure in the late nineties, but he rode it out, married Trina Abrams, and took a fundraising position with the Jewish Federation. If Mick ever dies, Jason will run Paley Lithwick.

✡

In the cabin, things were subdued. Normally, *nikayon* was a rowdy time of day that created more of a mess than it eradicated, but today the campers all made their beds, swept up, and folded their clothes without having to be told. Senior counselors stayed with one cabin all summer, while *machons* ro-tated to a new one every other week. We were expendable, the side dish you could ignore without going hungry. Every cabin but Rochelle's had one senior counselor and one *machon*. Hers had two senior counselors—Trina and Beth Ann Goldstein, a licensed social worker, approaching thirty years old, who took frequent trips to Milwaukee for some kind of appointment. We neither knew nor cared if she left to give treatment or receive it.

Since my arrival, Dallas Cowboy cheerleader Misty Norwood was our cabin's patron saint. My dad, who lived in Dallas, had mailed me an autographed poster, and I'd tacked it to the ceiling above my bed, with the idea of proving myself relatably horny—the kind of counselor who you could crack dirty jokes with. Misty's perfect, perfectly blonde hair and perfect, perfectly vacant countenance sanctified the space we inhabited. Oaths were sworn upon her breasts, which lurked beneath a white vest decorated with fringes and four blue Cowboy stars. To this day I occasionally Google-image "Misty Norwood" just to refresh my memory.

Doron normally insisted on blaring the three Billys—Billy Idol, Billy Joel (whose surname he pronounced with two syllables, accent on the second), and Billy "Stroke Me" Squier—but today he acceded to putting an Oingo Boingo cassette in the player, an oddly touching gesture since he was known to hate the new wave crap that Oliver adored. Or postpunk crap, as the boy took pains to point out. His kept his meticulously catalogued import-only releases in a faux leather attaché with a built-in combination lock. They were always rewound and returned to their proper cases after being played.

> There's nothing wrong with a mutation
> They're good for mankind and the nation,
> They're useful for society
> It breaks up the monotony!

Kyle Lombardi complained of a headache, but I discouraged him from visiting the infirmary. "You'll feel better after swimming," I said.

"Gee, thanks, Dr. Weintraub."

I looked away so as not to feel diminished by the boy's unearned yet effortless suavity, his pectoral muscles of a water polo champion, and his cheerful disregard for staff authority. Everything in his manner toward me conveyed *I bet you get laid a lot,* which made it awkward to command him to sweep the cabin floor.

The temperature climbed above 80 even before 9 a.m. The cloudless sky seemed to be airbrushed blue, and the batteries of the tape player must have been running low, because the music came out jerky and the pitch seemed to fluctuate.

✡

A hit-and-run storm had blown through the previous Sunday. Rochelle and I both had taken out kayaks. We hadn't been kayaking together, but we weren't far apart when a tall bank of charcoal clouds had rolled in from the west. Barometric pressure, a concept I understood but didn't quite trust, pushed against the walls of my inner ears. Invisible shapes churned beneath the surface of the water, tearing at my paddle. The rain and wind struck all at once, with more force than I'd ever experienced on land, and panic gripped me when the shoreline disappeared. Stronger and more efficient with the paddle, Rochelle maneuvered over to check on me.

Throwing me a nylon cord, she hollered, "Tie this around yourself" over the torrents, pantomiming the process. I nodded in understanding, but couldn't operate my hands at first. Eventually her encouragement paid off, and she began to tow me, but as the sheets of rain whipped harder, my agitated mind became convinced we were moving in the wrong direction. I called out to her, but she couldn't hear me or wouldn't turn around.

That's when I capsized. It may have happened because of my trying to scoot on my belly out onto the front of my boat to get her attention. The powerful waves rose up, the boat wobbled, and I slid off, trapping myself under the kayak. What had been panic transmuted into a detached paralysis. I remember marveling at the warmth of the water and wondering whether I was upside-down or not, and whether I was breathing air or not.

Naturally, because her kayak's rope was tied to my waist, I brought her down with me. Adding to my confusion was an instant when her kayak was nearly vertical. I didn't know where the horizon was anymore. Worse, I didn't particularly care.

The contortion of her milk-white face didn't initially register as laughter. At first I believed she was in pain, beseeching me for help. But then I saw she thought the storm and the capsizing were part of a terrific adventure. Camp bored her, and here was something that got the blood pumping. My numb face and addled speech enhanced the entertainment. I wasn't embarrassed, not until later. At the time I felt a kind of perverse pride in delighting her.

"How are you doing, birthday buddy?" she asked. The coursing rain had tamed her black ringlets.

"Wet," I answered.

Locking my gaze to hers in a kind of Vulcan-lifeguard hypnosis, Rochelle held onto me with one arm and to her inverted kayak with the other. The storm, which had taken mine, departed as quickly as it arrived. She told me about waterskiing, and how she wished the camp had a boat of its own, like the one the salesman had shown up with earlier. "It's hard at first, but then you feel as light as a breeze. You're alert and relaxed at the same time, just like the goddamn Buddha."

Sunbeams traced the contours of departing storm clouds. Soon my composure had returned enough that I could kick my feet and propel us to shore. We didn't discuss what happened, but I was determined to write a song about it. A song to show her my gratitude and to weave beauty out of near tragedy.

✡

My Hebrew class met at the foot a willow tree near the library. I passed out six distressed copies of *The Giving Tree,* and we took turns reading aloud. A strap of Tammy Hamelin's *beged-yam* kept sliding off her shoulder, but somehow I soldiered on.

"This is the most pathetic tree I ever heard of," Max sneered. "I would have told the boy to ram a branch up his ass by now."

"Why are we reading this book? Is Shel Silverstein even Jewish?"

"He's black I think. Ever see that picture of him on the back of *Where the Sidewalk Ends?* With the guitar and Afro and his big stinky foot held up at the camera?"

As we got to the part about the boy carrying away the tree's branches to build his house, I envisioned Rochelle in the passenger seat of a beat-up white van, her legs propped up on the dashboard. Where was the highway leading her, I wondered, and who was at the wheel? Had she been abducted, or was this a prison break that had been planned weeks in advance?

Oliver Berkowitz sat alone on the library steps, *Zen and the Art of Motorcycle Maintenance* balanced on his knee. Was it Rochelle's copy? The book had sold over 5 million of them. Assuming even a fifth of those copies had been read, that was roughly a shit ton of pseudo-philosophy being carried around in the bowels of our national consciousness. Oliver was not in my class, so it wasn't my concern where he was supposed to be during Hebrew.

"Does anyone remember how Hebrew conjugates the past tense?" I asked.

"How Hebrew *whats* the *what?*" Kyle complained. "It's like you're speaking a foreign language about a foreign language."

"What, *conjugate?*"

"Stop, you're making my headache worse. I thought this was supposed to be summer. Why did my parents have to send me to this yeshiva? Why can't we do the stuff normal camps do? Fishing, crossbows, wrestling. I want to build a massive bonfire and roast some pigs, not constipate Hebrew verbs."

"How do you say *sit?*" I tried again. Nobody spoke, so I answered my own question. "*Yoshev.*"

"Yo!" hooted Kyle, pointing at Tammy's stubbly underarm. "Shave!" As he withdrew his hand, one finger hooked the strap of her top, momentarily exposing 80 percent of one aureole. Her yelp contained both indignation and gratitude.

"Speaking of *yoshaving,*" Kyle said. "What's Oliver doing all the way over there? And why doesn't his forehead get any smaller when it's farther away?"

"It's called reading," Tammy answered. "Ever hear of books?"

"I read books," protested Kyle. "I read them all the time."

"I mean the kind without pictures."

I told the class that if they could plow through just three more pages, they could go to the lake early, but before we could go any further, Tammy cried out, "Goy alert!"

A fit man strode up to us wearing a red Izod tucked into pressed Levi's. He might as well have been carrying a placard that said "Plainclothes Wisconsin State Police."

"Eric Weintraub?" he said. I told the campers they should go to the lake.


# PART II

"The important thing is not to be afraid," advises Nachman. This instead of:

> *Don't look down*
> *Proceed swiftly*
> *Be careful with each step*
> *Be sure your pack is balanced*
> *Double-knot your shoelaces*
> *Don't overthink it*
> *Don't stop in the middle*

Telling people not to be afraid while crossing a narrow bridge is like throwing them in the sea and telling them not to drown. As far as I'm concerned, his advice is useless. Screw that guy.

Detective Hanekamp poured me a malodorous coffee in a Styrofoam cup and ran his fingers through his close-cropped blonde hair. We sat at a table in the great room of the Lodge, the only building at camp that could be called elegant, the facility where rabbis and other distinguished visitors stayed. Our table was positioned beside a picture window framing the winding limestone road that connected the Lodge to town.

"What can you tell me about Rochelle Strauss that I don't already know?" he asked. His biceps twitched like guinea pigs.

"Who else have you talked to?"

"Do me a favor, Eric. Let's have only one of us ask the questions."

"Am I in trouble?"

"And let's have the person be me."

The coffee tasted worse than it smelled. Was Rochelle dead? Did a trucker find her body in a ditch along the interstate? Was Rabbi Mick driving to Winnetka to deliver the news to the Strausses? I asked how I could help. He repeated his question.

"Not knowing what you know or don't know," I began. "Rochelle is fifteen years old. Her birthday was last week."

"And how old are you?"

"Seventeen. We actually have the same birthday."

"Isn't that special!" His blue eyes flashed. Not just Hanekamp, but Wisconsin itself, the world at large, had it in for the Jews. I resented his gentile intrusion onto our reservation.

"This is her first summer at camp, and she seems to like it, and everybody likes her."

"So I've gathered," the detective snorted.

"I don't know what you're getting at, but Rochelle is just a regular, sweet—"

"Beautiful, reckless daughter of a multimillionaire," he continued.

"I wouldn't know about any of that," I said, feeling left out of the universe that *reckless* implied.

"How would you describe her condition last night?"

"She seemed fine," I said, adding, "Her asthma was under control by the time I showed up."

"She wasn't upset?"

"No."

"Crying?"

"No."

"Anxious? Afraid?"

"It was dark," I said. "If she was any of those things, I couldn't have seen it."

In a manner calibrated to inform, not alarm me, Hanekamp laid out the urgency of locating missing persons within forty-eight hours of their disappearance. He told me about a teenage girl who ran away from Watertown and was picked up the same evening in the back of a Chinese restaurant whose owners said she reminded them of their dead daughter. They stayed friends with her for years and eventually paid her college tuition. Then he described another girl, a straight-A cheerleader from Menomonee Falls, who vanished on a Thursday and was found on a Saturday, dead of alcohol poisoning on the third floor of a University of Wisconsin-Stout fraternity house.

As he spoke, a Brunswick green Jaguar rolled in from town and pulled into a space outside the Lodge as I finished the last of the coffee. The Styrofoam was still warm and pliable, so I could turn the cup inside out, if I worked it patiently. Using both thumbs I applied pressure to the bottom.

"What did you talk about last night?"

"Nothing. I just told her to go back to her cabin. It wasn't a conversation."

"C'mon, Eric. Give me something to go on. If you can't help me out, I'm going to have to call in forty state troopers to drag the lake, and the only thing that will make them feel worse than finding a body is *not* finding a body and knowing they wasted their time because a junior counselor was trying to protect somebody."

"Nobody wants to find her more than I do," I said. "Find her alive, that is." The cup was halfway inside out. Rabbi Mick got out of the passenger side of the Jaguar. A fit woman in an expensive suit got out of the driver's side, but Detective Hanekamp either hadn't noticed or hadn't wanted to notice. "Tell me how to help. I want to help you find her."

"Let me ask you this," he said. "What do you think might have happened?"

"Could be a lot of things," I answered, wondering if he knew about Mick's scooter being gone and whether I should mention the time Rochelle had commandeered it.

"You're a responsible young man," Hanekamp said to me. "I might even go so far as to say you remind me of myself at your age."

"I'm actually supposed to collect my kids at the lake," I said, completing the inversion of the Styrofoam cup.

"Losing a camper probably wasn't what you signed up for," he continued. "I understand that, and you're handling it very well, all things considered."

Rabbi Mick and the woman walked in, and Mick's frown commanded my immediate departure. "You and I need to talk," the woman commanded Hanekamp, her features hard like a carved puppet's. Blonde, but not naturally, and a good fifteen years older than she first appeared, she moved swiftly but not fluidly. Each gesture comprised dozens of mechanical stages. I sidled out slowly enough to overhear her maintaining that the State of Wisconsin lacked jurisdiction in this matter. Hanekamp held his ground, and their voices rose as I let the door close behind me.

After that, the bottle blonde Mick had brought, who I learned was named Ms. Faber and represented the Strauss family, remained among us, a steadfast but enigmatic presence through lunch and afternoon programming. She stood off to the side, hands clasped behind her back, a half-smile chiseled on her face while we ate and sang and prayed. I heard campers guessing she was from the IRS, there to collect millions in back taxes. According to reliable sources, Paley Lithwick Strauss was going to be repossessed and converted to a casino.

"Think she's pretty?" Trina asked.

"Oliver says she's a hologram."

"I see you staring at her."

"Everyone's staring at her," I said. "We haven't had someone new to stare at in three weeks."

Occasionally Mick would enter the scene for a brief hushed conference. He would lean close to Faber, bouncing slightly on his toes, and she would pat him on the shoulder in a practiced reassuring, patronizing style before he darted away again. Doron nudged me. "Isn't that the sexy alien from that Indiana Jones movie?"

"Not an alien," I corrected. "A replicant."

"What difference does it make?" he said. "I want her. She wants me. It's just a matter of time before I'm waist deep in alien trim."

# PART III

*Erev Shabbat.* As the boys primped for dinner, the cabin smelled of talcum powder, Right Guard aerosol, and Polo cologne, but another spice was also woven into the atmosphere, too subtle to be identified just yet. New batteries in the tape player gave the Simple Minds extra punch. Oliver's parents had mailed him the cassette immediately upon its release.

> *Promised you a miracle*
> *Belief is a beauty thing*
> *Promises promises*
> *As golden days break wondering*

"You're not going to wear that, are you, Oliver?" Doron said, sniffing the air and frowning.

"What's wrong with it?"

"You can't wear a T-shirt on Shabbat. Especially not that."

Oliver held out the shirt so everyone could read *Fighting for Peace Is Like Fucking for Virginity.* "*Shalom* is *Shabbat*'s last name, right? It's a message of peace on the holiest day of the week. I don't see the big—"

"Don't make me tear it from your body." Naturally, a few of the boys whistled low at that.

Kyle retched. "What the hell is that? Does anybody else smell something that stinks like…?"

"Shit!" two or three campers finished his sentence for him. "It's Doron! Doron, it's you! What, did you forget to wipe or something?"

Doron plucked at his tank top to sniff the fabric, then twisted around in an attempt to catch a whiff of his own backside. His face crumpled in on itself as a paroxysm shook his entire frame, and the sound of ripping fabric filled the cabin. "Whoever did this, whoever *the fuck* did this…"

"Smell your pits!" someone shrieked.

Realization dawned on the red-faced Israeli, and he pulled the cap off his deodorant, pounced on Oliver, and pushed the stick into the boy's face.

"Think it's funny? Think it's *fucking* funny?"

"I didn't do anything!"

It took ten seconds too long, but I eventually remembered my responsibility to preserve order and tugged uselessly on Doron's shoulder. The smell of synthetic fragrance, sweat, rage, and whatever Oliver had rubbed into Doron's deodorant stick knocked me cross-eyed.

"Horse or human?" he glowered. "Just tell me if it's *horse or human* and I won't kill you right now in front of the whole cabin. It's not funny, I could catch a *serious* disease. Tell me *now*."

Flat on his back, but in a kind of rapture, the boy whinnied and let his eyelids flutter shut in expectation of a blow that never came. Doron stomped off to the shower, muttering a stream of Arabic curses. You had to admire his restraint.

At exactly 6:15 p.m., we lined up and met the girls in front of their cabins for clumsy hugging, but no kisses, so as not to disturb their Shabbat cosmetics. Their faces were noticeably less made up than usual, a change that I attributed to Faber. She must have paid a visit while the girls were readying themselves to give tips on blending eye shadow and to make a few subtle inquiries.

Mick lumbered up from the office to join us. It was odd to see him on foot like that, almost like Spiderman taking the stairs. Nobody mentioned Rochelle's absence, but it dented the space we moved through. The asthma story didn't fly anymore, probably never did. My guitar was slung over my back; the regular song leader was in Madison having his wisdom tooth removed. I worried about my first after-dinner song session falling flat, but I also wondered if I dared to perform, "Waking Up Our Dreams," one of three complete original compositions in my repertoire. (Years later a roommate pointed out that it plagiarized "Walking on the Moon" by The Police.) Trina took my arm as the procession swelled and curved around to the rotunda. "Shabbat Shalom, James Taylor."

"Hey," I breathed, bending my head down for a kiss that she reciprocated with surprising intensity. Her mouth tasted like cinnamon candy, and I could think of no reason not to see how things might progress between us after the campers went to bed. (There would be no Rat Fuck on Shabbat.)

At dinner we were talking about whether or not Faber was Jewish. Most of us said no, but Oliver insisted that he'd heard her utter a convincing *oy vey*.

"She doesn't look like a secretary."

"She's more than a secretary. Guys like Frankie Strauss have personal assistants who do a little bit of everything. The best ones are paid like professional athletes."

"Everything from hiring landscapers and mechanics to—"

"Scoring blow and hookers." To illustrate his point, Oliver cut a line of table salt and hoovered it up through one nostril. A sharp intake of breath was followed by a desperate glance to the left and right, and then his eyes squeezed shut. In a motion simultaneously improvised and calculated, he grabbed the loaf of challah from the table and sneezed into it.

"Out," came a foghorn voice. We all looked up into Rabbi Mick's take-no-prisoners black mustache.

"Where do I go?" Oliver whimpered, crumbs and snot stuck all over his face, from his famous forehead down to his glistening chin.

"Out," Mick repeated. "Now, you little homo peckerhead." (It would be wrong not to confess that this remark provoked general laughter—though in our defense, it was 1986—the sound of which must have followed the child as he slunk out of the dining hall, but not before grabbing a bottle of Mogen David by the neck.)

After the meal, the tables were cleared, and song session commenced, with me at the center strumming a bouncy march to welcome the Sabbath bride.

*Lecha dodi likrat kala, p'nei Shabbat n'kabelah!*

Continuing through a suite, traditional yet full of gusto, of "*Dodi Li,*" "*Al Hanissim,*" and "*Ma Gadlu,*" which had nearly everyone up and clapping. As I bobbed my head, droplets of sweat flew off me in slow motion and caught the beams of the setting sun.

Doron was doing a solo stationary rhumba. Girls had broken into groups of three and four to execute synchronized Marvelettes-like steps. Ms. Faber was seated but clapping beside Paley Lithwick's chief rabbi, Mordechai Y'raeh, a Holocaust survivor with a clubfoot, bilateral cataracts, and a permanent frown. It wasn't surprising that he wasn't clapping along, but every time I circled back near him his displeasure seemed to intensify. He looked like he was being forced to taste a bitter root.

As I swung into "*Ani Ma'Amin,*" the lower half of my body seemed to take on a life of its own, stutter-stepping and hip-swaying to beat the devil. Sixty voices came together into a raucous gospel, with every syllable stretched and syncopated. Caught up in the musical ecstasy swirling around me, I was self-aware enough to recognize how well this session was going. A vision popped into my mind of being promoted to first-string song leader. My technique was more than solid enough, my moves were impeccable, and my original material (maybe the song after next!) gave me an extra edge.

A sharp crack from the neck of my guitar slammed the brakes on our bacchanalia. At first it seemed like the instrument had spontaneously snapped in two, but then it became clear that Rabbi Y'raeh's walking stick had been swung with surprising might. His eyes burned into mine as a rushing silence filled my ears.

"*Emuna shlema, emuna shlema,*" he called out with Old Testament fervor. "Who can tell me what *emuna shlema* means?" Standing slightly askew, stooped yet defiant, the rabbi waited two beats for a response. "Perfect faith. *Perfect* faith. When you sing this song, you recite words that Rambam, the great Maimonides, penned eight hundred years ago. 'I believe with *perfect* faith in the coming of the Messiah, and, though he tarry, *I will wait* daily for his coming'.

"Ask yourselves if it's *tov* and *naim* to shake your pelvis and hiccup like a hound dog while you make this steadfast declaration of faith." Rabbi Y'raeh brandished his walking stick like a guitar and mocked the way I had shimmied around the floor. The laughter he earned resounded with the stockade. It occurred to me that I could be asked to pack my belongings and depart in the morning, so much violence had I committed to a core tenet of the Jewish religion. "'I believe with *perfect* faith in the coming of the Messiah, and, though he tarry, *I will wait* daily for his coming'," he repeated, "is one of the Thirteen Principles of Faith—the violation of even a single one of which prevents a Jew from reach *Olam ha-Ba,* the next world."

I hung my head and pretended not to notice the chip in the neck of my Washburn.

"Thank you, Rabbi," boomed Mick's voice as he took his place in the middle of the circle. "Thank you for that illuminating *parsha.* We are indeed fortunate to have such a wise teacher in our midst." Stunned campers and staff—all of whom, it became apparent, felt as guilty as I did—heaved a collective sigh of relief as Mick's familiar timbre displaced the real rabbi's *Polski* scolding. Mick began his customary pacing that announced he was about to tell a story. It was a ritual that even the hardest and least pious among us settled into like a bubble bath. I fell back and picked a gentle accompaniment as he began his tale.

> Rabbi Maimonides was indeed a great and inspired rabbi. This story concerns yet another figure from our rich heritage, Rabbi Hillel. Many of you probably know that when he was a young man, Hillel the Elder made his living as a woodcutter, and he made a humble home for himself in a cabin in the forest. He had not yet grown his famous beard.

I filled Mick's pause with the melody of "*Eitz chaim he,*" (it is a tree of life), which he acknowledged with the slightest, with a *nano* nod.

> Very early one Friday morning, Hillel set out with his axe and a broken-off piece of stale bread. He intended to cut

extra wood that morning, for the elder son of a neighboring family had fallen ill, and the great rabbi wanted to make sure the family could stay warm over the course of an unseasonably chilly Shabbat.

Like a catcher offering consultation to a reckless fastballer, Jason approached and feverishly whispered in his father's ear, but the advice went unheeded. I was close enough to hear the words "It's time they knew." His repertoire of stories was well known by many of us who had attended camp year after year. There was the one about the baker who left his village to dig up a treasure in Minsk. There was the one about the precious sapphire thought to be damaged forever when it cracked, until a mysterious visitor turned the flaw into a stem by chiseling the shape of a rose at one end. This one, however, was clearly new. Anticipation hummed through the room.

An enveloping mist gathered before dawn, making it extremely difficult for Hillel to see what he was doing. He had to rely on the echo of axe against wood to gauge his progress. Unfortunately, this meant he couldn't see a tree nymph who had been slumbering within an ancient cedar. The blade of his axe struck her in the thigh, and her scream of surprise and agony shattered the silence of the forest.

As I continued to improvise a dramatic melody of building intensity, I noticed Siggy VanderBeek, the camp's one-man maintenance crew, standing in the doorway, wearing his customary uniform of stained white overalls and backwards Utah Saints baseball cap. (According to an enduring and entirely unsupported rumor, there was a large swastika tattooed on his chest; hence the nickname Sig Heil.) He seemed to be watching me intently, but occupied as I was with my guitar figurings, I could not return his glance.

Though mostly encased in wood, the nymph had the face and body of a young girl, and real blood spilled profusely from her wound. With the sound of the flux harrowing his eardrums, Hillel started to unbutton his shirt in order to make a tourniquet from the fabric, but the nymph cried out, "Rabbi! You can still save my life if you act immediately."

"Anything at all!" he exclaimed. "Just tell me."

"The things that can stop me from dying are the three pillars of your faith," she moaned and then fell silent.

This was my musical cue. I adjusted the capo and launched into *"Al Shlosha D'varim,"* which enumerates the pillars upon which the world stands. Everyone from the youngest camper to Rabbi Y'raeh leaned in to find out what happened next.

> Hillel rushed back to his cabin and grabbed his most precious possession, a Torah scroll he had copied in his own hand when he was young. He placed it at the foot of the cedar, and soon the Holy parchment was saturated with nymph blood. *Torah* is the first pillar of the faith. The next pillar is *Avodah,* work. Woodcutting was the work Hillel knew best, so he proceeded to chop down every tree that encircled the wounded nymph. His muscles stung and he sweated blood, but he labored on until the sun was high in the sky.

Rabbi Mick stopped pacing and stroked his mustache, pausing as if to contemplate whether to reveal the rest of the tale. He seemed uncharacteristically shaken. I looked down at my hands and realized I had stopped playing.

> Hillel had made a clearing around the cedar tree. It was time to revive the nymph with the third pillar of our faith, *g'milut hasidim,* an act of lovingkindness. Unable to think of another course of action, the rabbi took his axe, which had been dulled from hours of chopping, and made a ragged incision in his own thigh. Intending, apparently, a kind of primitive blood transfusion, he pressed his open wound against hers. The earth trembled, for the tree was rooted to its core. The nymph's eyeballs swam to the back of her head in a kind of holy ecstasy, and she faded away, leaving the rabbi in the feverish embrace of the tree.
> Hillel awoke in his own bed, drenched, dazed, and bearded. The wound on his leg had healed, leaving behind a crescent-shaped scar. Three tall stacks of cedar logs stood outside his cabin in the morning sun.

Thinking the story was over, Siggy beckoned to me, but I sensed Rabbi Mick had more to tell and waved the maintenance man off.

> Several hundred years later, a Jewish young man wandered the forest, daydreaming about what fate might hold in store when a stench nearly overpowered him. Hundreds of dead and dying woodland mammals encircled a giant cedar

tree standing alone in a rust-colored pond. Always curious, Jonas collected a sample of the water and rushed home to examine it under a homemade microscope.

My fingers had gone arthritic, or the guitar strings had become too far away from each other, because I couldn't seem to form a simple chord. I attempted tapping a jaunty rhythm on the body of the instrument, but Mick shot me a look and I put my hands on my cocked hips, imagining myself looking at least a tad Keith Richards-ish.

The man with the microscope was named Jonas Salk, later world famous for inventing the polio vaccine made of dead cells. People were afraid this Jewish researcher would poison them, so before testing the vaccine more broadly, he injected himself, his wife and his three sons after boiling the needles and syringes on the stovetop of the kitchen in his home. Having proved the injections safe, he spread the formula widely, refusing to take out a patent—for, as he told a reporter, "Could you take out a patent on the sun?" The dead viruses he put into the serum run through all your veins today. Without his discovery, at least a third of you would be helpless cripples.

Campers and counselors alike remained seated, stunned, and silent. Tammy Hamelin, Trina Abrams, and the mysterious woman hired by the Strauss family rocked together in a tearful huddle. I finally stepped into the corridor to see what Siggy wanted. "That cop showed up and told me to give you this," he said, holding out the inverted Styrofoam cup.

# PART IV

Campers asleep, supposedly, Trina and I made out in the gazebo just a few hundred feet from the girls cabins. The sky was black, and the air was sultry and still as we intermittently plotted our Talent Show duet.

"Wanna wear matching costumes?" she asked.

"Are you kidding? This is James and Carly, not Sonny and Cher." In response to her empty stare, my hand found its way to her bare kneecap.

"By the way," she said, "I told Faber about us, and she wants to hear it."

"Has she told you anything she hasn't told the campers?"

"She doesn't *tell*. She listens. She keeps her mouth shut, and the girls line up to bust out every Rochelle fact and myth for her. At most, she replies, 'I see'." Trina didn't push my hand away but instead did some ambiguous re-positioning. "Every so often she jots a note down in this Trapper Keeper thing she carries with her. What Rochelle said about her family. Who were her favorite and least favorite counselors. Where she went at night. I went through her laundry bag today without even being asked to. It's like she's the perp rather than the victim."

"What'd you find?"

Her dark eyes flashed. "It's laundry. What do you think I found? Un-derpants. Wait here, Eric, I'll fetch them so you can have a whiff."

This wasn't going as planned. We weren't supposed to be talking about Rochelle, but then how could we talk about anything else? Wherever we looked, there she wasn't. I learned that she'd been leaving her cabin almost every night since camp began, often placing collect calls from the forbidden payphone in the back of the Lodge. Some girls said she called her mom; others claimed it was a married man she'd been seeing, the father of her best friend. More than one girl swore she had a talent agent in Hollywood who was this close to getting her cast opposite Rob Lowe in the sequel to *Oxford Blues*.

"What about Mick?" I asked.

"That man, I swear, he seems more worried about his shiny red Vespa than his missing camper. It's one of the sources of his power, the ability to glide all over camp while the rest of us mortals walk. What was up with that story tonight?"

"There are going to be nightmares about axes—guaranteed."

"And Jason!" she exclaimed, but her voice trailed off into regret.

"What about him?"

"Nothing, he just seems really upset by all this. I mean we're all upset, but he's maybe a little more upset than he should be."

"What do you m—"

"Nothing, I don't want to keep talking anymore. Did you know your lips are much prettier when they're not flapping around so much?"

I complied, but the purpose of the kiss was clearly shutting me up, so it didn't feel as good as it should have with the words I wanted to speak were locked inside.

Trina half-whispered half-moaned something that sounded suspiciously like *I love her*, to which I almost responded *I love her too*.

"Oliver," she enunciated more clearly this time. "What do you need?"

"Eric," said the boy, looking disappointed at our frivolous necking. He had more desperate matters to address. "Can I show you something?"

I detached myself from Tina and pulled my T-shirt down over the jut-ting in my shorts. "Good," she smiled, "you've brought your flashlight." And she sauntered away.

Oliver's already pale face was completely drained of color, except for the raccoonish shadows tracing his eye sockets. Recovering from my irritation at being interrupted, I realized that he was genuinely distressed. "Did something happen?"

"It's hard to explain. I need to show you."

"Does Doron know you're out of the cabin?"

"Doron? He's too proud of himself to notice something he wouldn't have noticed anyway."

"Proud of what?"

"The discovery of a new passage to female ecstasy. Totally perverted. He's calling himself Christopher Clitoris."

We skirted the camp property line that ran alongside the Lodge, past a scrub of crab apple bushes. He wasn't very good at leading, possibly because he was torn between the urgency of his mission and his reluctance to arrive where we were going. The sweet kosher wine he had undoubtedly consumed may also have impaired his step. We kicked crabapples out of our way and almost tripped over each other's feet as we moved through the darkness. Oliver's wine-scented breathing was irregular, punctuated with gravelly whistles.

"You okay?"

"Just a little further. Could you turn your flashlight on now?"

"My what?"

"Trina said you…oh, ha, never mind." The hot night invited swarms of invisible insects that died on contact with sweaty skin. The underbrush clung to our bare legs.

By the way," I said. "Have you noticed anything unusual about Jason Harris lately?"

"He does seem a little…preoccupied."

"Like how?"

"Like staring into space without the staring. His eyes address the void with his hand against his cheek like Jack Benny. Do you think Mick let him know what's going on?"

"What *is* going on, Oliver?" I asked.

"Tammy says they're getting permission from the family to open the package." Not knowing what he was referring to but not wanting to reveal my ignorance, I made a noncommittal sound, something between a grunt and mmm-hmm, and hoped he would continue.

"Would it be okay if I just show this to you without describing it? I want to get your advice about what to do, but I don't want to have to get into how I found it or what I know or don't know about how it got there."

"What do you think I can do about it?"

"I don't have any idea," he said, near tears. "That's the whole problem. Maybe we should just forget it."

"Oliver," I said. "Is this regular serious or really really serious? If it's, like, legal, I may not be able to keep a promise of secrecy."

He scoffed. "I'm not leading you to Rochelle Strauss's dismembered corpse, if that's what you're thinking," and a long sigh of relief rose from the depths of my lungs.

We came to a clearing that was starlit enough that, after a few seconds, what Oliver had to show me came into focus. It was dismembered, but it was not a corpse at all. The parts were metal and painted a glossy red.

"Fucking A, Oliver."

"Ever use the last stall in Noah's ark?" he said dreamily. "The one that says, 'Those who write upon the walls / Roll their shit into little balls. / Those who read these words of wit / Eat the little balls of shit."

"Sure, but this is what you wanted 'advice' about? Advice isn't going to help you here. Not one bit. My advice is to not seek advice anymore."

"You know what Zoroaster said? 'A knife of the keenest steel requires the whetstone, and the wisest man needs advice'."

"Yeah, well, he was wrong."

When Oliver hiccupped, I could hear the tears coming. "Remember the night of the Rat Fuck, when he made everyone vote whether to send me home or not? After that I pushed the scooter out here. He's a tyrant who preys on the weak." When I neither agreed nor disagreed, he added. "I want to be a shit roller, not a shit eater."

"You're more of a bread-sneezer."

"Har har. I couldn't help it. But what he said was unforgiveable. That's when I came back here with a screwdriver and a wrench."

I don't know how long we stood in the clearing. Rabbi Mick's scooter, one of the main sources of his power over us, lay scattered all around in the unmowed grass. I was just as scared of him as Oliver was, just as unwilling to go to him with the information. Staying with the evidence was dangerous. Walking back to camp invited risks of its own. What if someone spotted us and asked where we'd been?

I pictured the scrawny pre-adolescent coming here after being ejected from the dining hall, dismantling the bike in the Wisconsin twilight. His determination awed me, despite his subsequent loss of nerve.

"Fucking A," I said, and we exchanged smiles.

If I was an accessory to the crime, so was Trina. She had heard Oliver saying he wanted to show me something. I could say it was a rash on his groin. Or I could tell her. Or I could show her. She was more mature, more capable of handling a crisis like this than I was.

"I'll take care of this," I assured him.

"What does that mean?"

"I don't have a clue, actually." We made our way back without another word spoken. Nobody saw us, and when we got back to the cabin, all the campers were sleeping and so was Doron Ba'al Shem Tov, aka Christopher Clitoris, a vagina's worth of short curlies under each arm, a plastic bag spilling mini bagels next to his bed. His broad, dark brown chest rose and fell, rose and fell. He managed to look contemptuous and lewd even in sleep.

Oliver stepped out of his shorts and stood over him. The spindly silhouette of his naked lower half stood out against the murky darkness. There wasn't enough light to see the look on his face, but his posture was somehow more menacing than his physique. I sank into my bed as he sniffed his briefs, nodding in appreciation before daintily draping them over the hated counselor's face.

# PART V

The theme of the Shabbat morning service was "courage," led by the girls cabin that wasn't missing anybody. Between prayers, the campers took turns reading original meditations out loud. My guitar rested on my knee unplayed as I half-listened to subliterate adolescent notions of courage.

*Webster's Collegiate Dictionary defines 'courage' as the mental or moral strength to venture, persevere, and withstand danger, fear, or difficulty. Normally, we think that courage is a quality shown only by heroes in books, but every single one of us has the seeds of courage deep inside of us.*

*The Jews of Masada showed courage when they took their own lives rather than allowing their enemies conquer them. Please rise for the Bar'chu*

*The Jews in the Warsaw Ghetto Uprising showed courage when they rose up against their Nazi oppressors even though they were outnumbered. Please rise for the Sh'ma.*

*Abraham Joshua Heschel wrote, "A mitzvah is an act in which we go beyond the scope of our thought and intention." That's what courage is to me.*

*The tree in Shel Silverstein's "The Giving Tree" ...*

The girls continued as Mordechai Y'raeh stood and limped out of the chapel.

*Charlotte in "Charlotte's Web"...*

*Elliot shows courage when he helps E.T. go home...*

*The founders of the State of Israel...*

I suddenly remembered that right after services I was supposed to lead a small group session on Israel but still hadn't found an article for discussion. There was just enough time to slip into the library to pick up some material. Luckily, it was unlocked. Neither Leon Uris's *Exodus,* nor Moshe Dayan's memoirs, nor Saul Bellow's *To Jerusalem and Back* captured my attention. Chaim Potok's *Wanderings* had some unshakeable negative associations that predated my earliest memories. I found a legal pad and scribbled groups of words that might coalesce into lyrics for my song for Rochelle.

*Rescue / Thank you*
*Storm / Warm / Calm*
*Grip / Slip / Lips*

Awful. If and when she came back, she deserved better than that. How would Bob, Paul, and Leonard do it? Did they use rhyming dictionaries? Did they clutch their instrument to their bosoms waiting for the spirit of King David to bestow upon them a new song? In search of inspiration, I pulled down an anthology of Jewish women poets, a manual on water rescue, and a meteorology textbook. Back then, I didn't read books. I ravished them in pursuit of lyrics, rifling the pages and folding down corners, underscoring lines and scrawling in the margins.

Paul Simon grew up loving Elvis Presley, in Forest Hills, Queens, a place I invested with magic, just as Simon did with Tupelo, Mississippi. Art Garfunkel was his best friend in middle school. They started out as teen pop sensations Tom and Jerry before reclaiming their ethnic surnames and blessing America with their full-bodied songs. I didn't need a girlfriend, I reflected. I needed a best friend, a Garfunkel of my own. Trina Abrams? Oliver Berkowitz? Weintraub and Berkowitz wasn't a name destined for the charts.

The meteorology book had a cool diagram of cloud formations that I contemplated tearing out before remembering the Xerox machine. Fortunately, someone had left an article about Israel on the glass plate, so that solved my *limudim* problem.

The lilac paperback, Robert Pirsig's bestselling *Zen and the Art of Motorcycle Maintenance,* lay in the return bin.

The rack of film canisters leaning against one wall reminded me that I was also responsible for picking a Saturday night movie. The camp owned fifty or so, but we always seemed to watch *Grease, The Russians Are Coming,* or *The Fiddler on the Roof.* I was contemplating Neil Diamond's version of *The Jazz Singer* when I realized I was not alone.

"Are you a camper or a counselor?" I whirled around to find Ms. Faber seated with a flaming orange copy of *Time* magazine—Meltdown: Chernobyl Reactor. Her voice sounded like someone doing a bad impersonation of either Mae West or Billie Holiday. She wore a charcoal silk smock, matching culottes, and tooled leather ankle boots. Didn't she remember me from the

Lodge with Detective Hanekamp? The binder that Trina had mentioned lay flat on the table.

"I'm a *machon*. That is, a junior counselor," I answered, and told her my name. She asked how I liked camp and how long I had been going, but for the most part, just as Trina had described, she kept her mouth shut.

"I just finished Glenbrook North," I said, stuffing my guitar case pocket with the paperback, the movie, and copies of the article.

"You live in Northbrook?"

"I did, but we moved, my mom and I. We moved to Morton Grove in September, but they left me finish up at GBN."

"And are you going to University of Illinois like everyone else?"

"*Northern* Illinois, actually."

"I see." That carefully tousled pixie cut probably cost more than I was being paid for the entire summer. Frank Strauss's wealth emanated off her like cold from an industrial air-conditioner.

What did Strauss actually do to make all his money? Mick said it was buying companies that were about to go out of business. This idea circled my brain without finding an entrance. Say you take over a dry cleaner or a car manufacturer or something—then what? Was he so good that he could make a business turn a profit where nobody else could before? Did he spiff up the books and sell to another fool? Did he find buyers for the equipment, the building, and the unsold merchandise? None of these strategies seemed like a recipe for millions.

Fortunes could be made, if you just knew what to do. Education and hard work were the best-known paths, but neither was my strong suit. Making something from nothing, that appealed to me. A hit record. Maybe an invention or a business deal. Power made money. Knowledge made money. Money made money. I lacked all these things, as well as the greed that made them go.

Faber probably knew my family situation better than anyone else at camp, maybe even better than I knew myself. She also knew that I was the last person to see her boss's daughter before the disappearance, but she wasn't going to directly interrogate me. It was more economical to let me prattle on. Had she spoken to Oliver? If so, had he reported the shit that Doron and I had talked in Noah's Ark? Would "Blowchelle" be my undoing? She probably neither knew nor cared about Mick's scooter, but a cold sweat covered me at the recollection of its pieces scattered in the grass.

"Yeah, even though I finished early, I had sort of a lot of incompletes. Bit of a perfectionist, I guess. There was this biography assignment, and I chose Richard J. Daley. Before long I had read a thousand pages and produced over two hundred pages of notes, but I couldn't seem to shape them into a ten-page paper."

"I see."

"Yeah, I'm more into songwriting, actually. My brother's the brains in the family. He's going to be a junior at Yale."

"E.L.? Where's that?"

"No, *Yale*. As in Harvard and."

"I see."

"Hey," I said, finally mustering the strength to change the subject. "I've got to get to *limudim,* that is, Jewish study. Would you like to sit in? We're talking about Israel."

# PART VI

I explained to Faber that it was the same group I had for Hebrew, in the same place, but instead of studying the language we read a short article on a Jewish theme and had a discussion about it. She pulled a Burberry scarf out of her bag so she could sit with us on the grass. I didn't introduce her and she didn't introduce herself.

The article was about the latest chapter in the Arab-Israeli conflict. Considering how I'd stumbled across it, I was pleased that it seemed to address a bunch of current topics at once. Previous sessions had covered the Balfour Declaration, the War for Independence, the Six-Day and Yom Kippur Wars, and the peace treaty with Egypt, so I thought it made sense to get up to date on the Holy Land. Camper participation in these discussions never got particularly animated, but my main concern was holding Faber's interest.

We took turns reading paragraphs aloud. Kyle wanted to know where Lebanon was, and I sent him to the library for a map. Faber asked for a show of hands of who had been to Israel, a sensitive topic for me. I had planned to go that summer on a trip sponsored by Chicago Suburban Jewish Youth, but my mother had failed to mail the deposit, in spite of all my reminders and all her promises. It was one of a series of failures that had led my father to consider returning from Dallas for an extended period, but ultimately he couldn't get away from a big parking garage real estate deal he was overseeing.

But Faber couldn't have known about that, right?

Tammy Hamelin hadn't been to Israel, but a *goyische* ex-boyfriend used to say the whole idea of it was like asking half the world's Jews to wear a big target that said "Bomb Me" on it in big letters.

"Was it uncircumcised, Tammy?"

"Why didn't they just put Israel in Skokie, where all the Jews are anyway?" said Kyle, returning from the library.

"There's this thing called the Western Wall," sneered Max Newmark. "It's sort of famous, and guess what, it's in Jerusalem."

"So?"

"So Jerusalem is in Israel. Right, Kyle? You have the map."

Tammy popped her bubblegum. "It's like one big Rat Fuck in the desert."

"Tammy!"

"I'm sorry, but it is. Israel and Palestine are like these two cabins right next to each other. One of them shouts one thing, and the other gets mad and shouts something worse. If the first cabin doesn't come back with a really terrible insult, it's a sign of weakness, so it goes on and on, until a counselor shows up—that's the U.N., obviously—and says the Rat Fuck has to stop or nobody gets pizza."

"What's the pizza?" asked Kyle.

"The pizza is all the things we give Israel: tourism, foreign aid, walk-a-thons, whatever."

"Tammy ordered extra cheese," laughed Kyle.

"I think what we have right here," I said, "is a very thought-provoking metaphor."

"Let's say Lady Smegma is right, and it is all one big Rat Fuck," Max argued. "It didn't just come out of nowhere, did it? Somebody Rat Fucked first. That's obviously the P.L.O. They bomb a bus, we blow up a town. They take a hostage, we imprison fifty suspects. Do you really think that if we suddenly stop Rat Fucking them they'll stop Rat Fucking us? I guarantee you, we stop Rat Fucking them for a minute, they Rat Fuck us into the Mediterranean."

Faber stood up and walked away.

"What was *that* about?"

"Maybe she had reached her quota of four-letter words."

"Maybe she's still offended by Eric's pelvic-thrusting '*Ani Maamin*'. Besides, smegma is six letters."

"Maybe she has Rabbi Mick bound and gagged in the office."

Trying not to look at Tammy, I asked, "Did you guys hear about a care package that came for Rochelle yesterday?" but Kyle and Max were too enthralled by the idea of Mick tied to his office chair that they ignored the question. Until the end of *limudim,* we continued to speculate on the many torments in store for the camp director.

✡

*Fiddler on the Roof* was more like a family heirloom quilt than an ordinary motion picture. It conformed to our bodies and our hearts. Each tune confirmed something essential about our identity as American Jews. It was a comfort to know every line before it was uttered, especially because the audio left much to be desired. I had the honor of prying open the canister and threading the film through the antique projector.

"Come on, Weintraub, slip it in!"

"Don't jab. Be gentle."

"Is it even stiff enough?"

It took a steady hand and determination to persist while impatience seethed all around me. Everyone wanted their Saturday night movie. At last, the *shtetl* rooftops loomed into view and the mysterious fiddler began sawing away.

"Jump! Jump!"

As the foldout screen swallowed the fat flickering light, some campers continued to blurt out comments while others took advantage of the dimmed lights for amorous purposes. I stood in the back of the Orlove Saxton Activity Center, known by all as Oralsex, noting who was paired off this week. It was spread out before me like a Hieronymus Bosch painting, the sensual back massages, the fingertips tracing figure eights on pulse points, the earlobe nibblings, the chubby hands inching along inner thighs and into loose waistbands. The message of *Fiddler,* that true love between a boy and a girl is the highest power, as long as the boy and the girl are both Jewish, poured over the roiling mass of sleeping bags like rain falling on parched earth.

Tammy Hamelin, who was almost always entangled with some boy or another, sat by herself, almost prim, with hair pulled back in a tangerine scrunchy. She wore a Fighting Illini sweatshirt, with the neck hole ripped out, made of fabric thick enough to mask those weapons-grade nipples. The light reflecting off the movie screen made her face look like a black-and-white photograph. It was more beautiful, in a way, than Rochelle's, which was already receding into an icon of memory. Undoubtedly, every one of us thought about Frank Strauss and his Winnetka mansion while Tevye sang "If I Were a Rich Man," but we kept it to ourselves.

Around the time of Tevye's nightmare, I exited Oralsex, not caring if the film reel snagged. In back of the Lodge, I pulled out the paperback that Oliver and maybe Rochelle had been reading, and dialed a number that had been written in ballpoint in a feminine hand on the inside back cover.

"It's you again, ay?" came a gruff voice.

"I don't think so," I replied.

"Then it probably isn't. Who are you looking for?"

"I was hoping you could do me a favor."

"Doing favors is kind of my specialty, ay?" There was a sound of liquor pouring into a small glass with ice.

"Do you know Detective Hanekamp?"

"Chris Hanekamp? He used to be married to my cousin. I know him."

"Can you tell him I'll meet him at ten tonight? Tell him Eric from camp."

"Eric Hanekamp?"

"No, Eric *from* the *camp.*"

"The Jewish camp?"

"Yes."

"*Shavuah Tov,* Eric." The phone went dead and I went to the cabin. The lights were off, but as soon as I opened the door it was obvious I didn't have the place to myself. For one thing, it smelled like a construction site outhouse. For another, there was Doron, hunched over Oliver's tape player. Beside him on the bed was a roll of Scotch tape and a Zip-Loc bag with a few gray crumbs left.

I watched as he removed a Bauhaus cassette from Oliver's prized faux-leather music holder and popped open the case. Methodical yet clumsy, he tore off a piece of tape and covered the small indentations on the top.

"What is this?" I asked.

"Shrooms give me gas," he answered, as if that clarified anything. He rewound the tape to "She's in Parties" and let the ominous, pounding music fill the room for a few seconds.

> *Freeze frame screen kiss*
> *Hot heads under silent wigs*
> *Fall guys tumble on the cutting room floor*
> *Look-a-likes fall on the cutting room door*

Doron hit "stop" and then simultaneously pressed "play" and "record," winking at me and releasing a long, low fart. I told him it was a very original form of music criticism. "I prefer to think of it as a collaboration," he answered. "It's a great honor to perform this duet with Bauhaus. I've also added my personal sonic touch to the Sisters of Mercy, the Colourfield, and Shriekback." He ejected the Bauhaus and replaced it with Ultravox's *Systems of Romance.*

> *I turn around to switch the scene*
> *The room dives like a submarine*
> *I cross the carpet trying to leave*
> *Sometimes I can do it*
> *When you walk through me*

"Can I have one of those bagels?" I said, pointing to the sack beside his bed.

"No, those are stale, and besides, they aren't for eating."

"Then what—"

"Wait! That's the cue for my solo," he declared, before producing a ferocious polysyllabic skronk.

"Come with me to Yon Yonson's tonight," I said. "I'm meeting someone."

"How are we going to get there?"

"Can't you borrow Steve S's car?"

"For some reason he's been downright unfriendly toward me lately."

"For some reason?"

"For some reason he didn't like it when I ate all his shrooms. What about Trina? She has that yellow Gremlin, and you guys are a thing now, right?"

We planned to meet at the camp gate at 9:45 as Doron found the opening yowl of the Cult's "She Sells Sanctuary." I crouched down low, the better to add my own A-flat bugle note to his final *shofar* blast.

# PART VII

Trina did have that yellow Gremlin, but I didn't want her coming to Yon Yonson's —nor did I want her to know I was going to Yon Yonson's. Not a single convincing reason came to me, but first I had to put the boys to sleep. Over the previous few nights I had read them T. H. White's *The Once and Future King,* which my counselors had read to me, but this group was aggressively not into it, so I decided to try some Pirsig, casually mentioning that Rochelle had been seen with this very copy the night she disappeared.

> *Laws of Nature are human inventions, like ghosts. Laws of logic, of mathematics are also human inventions, like ghosts. The whole blessed thing is a human invention, including the idea that it isn't a human invention. The world has no existence whatsoever outside the human imagination. It's all a ghost, and in antiquity was recognized as a ghost, the whole blessed world we live in. It's run by ghosts. We see what we see because these ghosts show it to us, ghosts of Moses and Christ and the Buddha, and Plato, and Descartes, and Rousseau and Jefferson and Lincoln, on and on and on. Isaac Newton is a very good ghost. One of the best. Your common sense is nothing more than the voices of thousands and thousands of these ghosts from the past. Ghosts and more ghosts. Ghosts trying to find their place among the living.*

"Eric?"

"Yeah Max?"

"Can we go back to King Pellinore tomorrow? No offense to Rochelle, but whatever that was didn't even bore me enough to make me fall asleep."

Afterward, I lingered outside the cabin waiting for anyone but Trina to happen by. It was an ideal opportunity to eavesdrop on the lights-out conversation within, presumably the kind of bull session on God that had nourished my mind when I was a camper. I couldn't imagine these kids ever saying things like "God is a mystery, but the mystery is not God."

"I'm telling you, there was something stuffed into that Speedo."

"But you can't fake muscles like that. Especially in a Speedo."

"He looked like Rick Springfield."

"You *would* notice that, Berkowitz. Did you ask if you could massage suntan oil into his shoulders while he sang 'Jesse's Girl'?"

"She was just really into waterskiing. After two tries she was barefooting it."

"That waterski guy was a total butt slammer, so, no, he didn't whisk our Rochelle away."

"Did you hear him telling her he knew her dad somehow?"

"Guys," interrupted Kyle, "I probably shouldn't be telling you this, but here goes."

"Those are invariably the exact words he uses before telling us a lie."

"Shut up. Rochelle and I were totally having a super-intense secret romance the last few days before she disappeared."

"I thought you were still with Evie."

"This was after that. Every night *before* lights out Evie and I would go into a *kita* and jack each other off, but I'd make her stop just before I came. She begged to finish me off, but I explained it would crimp my water polo game."

"Evie's the second hottest girl in this camp. Half the male counselors and at least two female counselors have made a pass at her."

"Yeah, but I was saving my spunk for the hottest girl."

"This is bullshit."

"No, I swear to God. You guys can't tell anybody. Rochelle and I had been meeting *after* lights out and doing it in the chapel like dogs."

As canine howls sounded, my face grew hot.

"I mean it," he said. "Actual dogs couldn't have improved on our style."

"When she comes back, I am totally going to ask her about this."

"*If,* you mean."

"This has to be a total secret," Kyle continued. "I don't want that FBI lady giving me the third degree."

"One phone call and she could have you locked up."

"They're both minors. It's not a crime."

"We're talking about Rochelle Strauss, daughter of the richest Jew in the Chicagoland area. You'll be doing it like dogs with a guy named Diego."

"That's *if* there's a shred of truth to his shaggy dog tale, which I seriously doubt."

"Suck it, Max. You've noticed me walking funny, right? Now you know why. Rochelle Strauss was out of control. It was like canine revenge sex from Mars. I had to put my hand over her mouth so her moans wouldn't be heard."

✡

Kyle has built a prestigious sports medicine practice, his Gold Coast office predictably bedizened with jock memorabilia. Everywhere he goes, even temple, he wears about five pounds of gold. He cruises the burbs in a yellow Lamborghini with "SCORE1" plates. His wife instructs mine in pilates; his kids pretend to be friendly with mine. A few years ago, the family of a deceased Chicago Blackhawk won a seven-figure malpractice case against Kyle and his partner, and the *Sun-Times* ran a headline gloating "Sports Docs Sent to Penalty Box," but the ordeal didn't noticeably humble him. When he and I periodically cross paths, he always tries enticing me to join up with a group of guys on a Las Vegas junket. "I've actually never been to Vegas," I admit. "You kidding me?" he replies. "You'd love it." I always say I'll let him know.

Max is a veterinary ophthalmologist and Scrabble champion.

✡

I was saved from the prospect of going back inside by Jason Harris emerging from his cabin, looking unsteady. He wobbled a few steps in the direction of the Lodge (momentarily causing me to wonder if he, too, had been screwing Rochelle) and then stood still with an unfocused gaze stamped on his face. "You okay?" I asked, startling him partially out of his reverie.

"Eric? Yeah, I'm good. But is it okay if we skip the bar mitzvah tonight, because I am just not up for that right now."

"Nothing would make me happier."

"Then can I show you something?"

"You too?"

"What does that mean?"

"Nothing, it's just that somebody just asked me that same question last night." It came as a shock that my nighttime walk with Oliver took place only twenty-four hours earlier. So much was happening, and yet all of it was already beginning to feel natural—Rochelle's absence, Faber's presence, the veil of suspicion that covered each and every one of us.

"Is the projector still set up?"

"Yeah," I said. "Feel like watching *Fiddler* again?"

"Yes, I mean no." he said. "Let's go to Oralsex." He held up a small, new-looking film canister.

Jason told me not to tell anyone, but Paley Lithwick was facing financial scrutiny like never before. Ever since the Strauss gift, his dad was under pressure to boost sagging revenue. Competitors in the region screened "happy camper" movies for groups of parents shopping around for the most enriching summer experiences, so he had ordered a bunch of new film equipment in order to make a marketing documentary of his own. Jason had been testing out the camera when an idea struck him. The documentary could wait. This was his chance to make a really amazing portfolio reel so he could transfer to USC.

"And we have only one movie star at this camp, right? It didn't take much to persuade her." He dimmed he lights and threaded the reel expertly, making me wonder why he hadn't relieved me of my embarrassed fumbling earlier in the evening.

"She only asked if she could use the reel too, to send to this agent friend of her aunt. Her parents wanted her to wait until after graduation, but she was afraid that if she waited that long she'd get fat like her mom."

"So you think…"

"Maybe she decided it would be better to show up in person. And the whole thing would have been my idea."

The screen came alive with light, the hand-lettered title *Road Block* scrolling up from below. On a silent, black-and-white summer day, a girl pedals her bike down a limestone path. (The filmmaker must have rolled alongside on his dad's scooter, because she stays pretty much in the center of the picture as the landscape flows past.) Her face is placid as she rises in the seat and increases speed. (Either it is not, after all, a face made to be immortalized in celluloid, or else the right director of photography has yet to bless it; she looks younger and less symmetrical than she does in person.) The tulle skirts of a wedding gown are hiked up to her thighs. With one hand, she holds what remains of a veil to keep it from blowing off. All of a sudden in close-up, she looks troubled and applies the brakes. Dismounting, she stumbles to a black casket lying in the road (a prop I recognized from previous theatrical productions—same as the wedding dress), throws it open, and collapses in tears. Her narrow shoulders tremble. (This gesture is genuinely, movingly cinematic. Her every movement obeys the dictates of silent film.) A clever jump cut reveals the inside of the casket—Rochelle herself, her face fixed in a rictus of simulated death.

Then came a "The End" sign, followed by:

| Director | J. Howard Harris |
| Girl on bike | Rochelle La Vraie |

His statement was self-evident. We had only one movie star at this camp, and that was Rochelle. What did that make Jason, me, any of us? We were bit players. That was perfectly acceptable. The most important thing was playing my part to the hilt.

Jason sighed. "She was like, 'In my family, all the women's butts blow up to five times their girlhood size on our eighteenth birthdays'." He began to further explain, unnecessarily, that Howard was his middle name and that Strauss would never survive Hollywood, when Trina came up behind us. Either Jason had somehow flipped off the projector before she noticed what we were watching, or else she chose not to comment. "You two getting ready for Eric's big night?"

"Speak of the devil," I said, cracking myself up more than Jason.

"We need to postpone the festivities," Jason said. "My dad asked us to cool it with the *b'nei mitzvah* for a while."

"Faber?"

"Faber. That woman is a walking fun-eraser."

"Okay!" she smiled. "At least we can practice 'Mockingbird,' Eric."

"Actually, I need to get out of here," I said.

Trina folded her arms. "Weren't you just watching a movie with Jason? I want to see it, too. Or is it some kind of porno?"

"Starring Ms. Faber," I said.

"And the biggest horse in the stable," Jason added. "Actually, it's a documentary about Catherine the Great."

Doron was waiting for me, but she loathed him, so I couldn't mention his name. "Trina, can I borrow your car tonight?"

"Before I say no, when are we going to practice? The Talent Show is tomorrow night."

"Tomorrow before dinner, promise."

"So what's the big emergency?"

"Nothing really," I said, "just my mom." I had sketched some of my family drama for her, mainly to elicit a particular variety of emotional capital, and now seemed like a good time to cash in.

"Where?" she asked, suddenly sympathetic.

"Menomonee Falls," I said, remembering the name of a nearby town that Hanekamp had mentioned. "In a Holiday Inn. She sounded kind of sleepy on the phone."

# PART VIII

The Gremlin idled at the camp gate, which had recently gained a Strauss besides its Paley and Lithwick shingles. If I waited much longer for Doron I'd risk being late for my meeting with Hanekamp. Squeeze was back in the tape deck.

> *My eagle flies tomorrow*
> *It's a game I treasure dear*
> *To seek the helpless future*
> *My love at last I'm here*
> *Take me I'm yours*
> *Because dreams are made of this*
> *Forever there'll be*
> *A heaven in your kiss*

50

I scolded myself for not having praised Jason's directorial prowess. He had taken me into his confidence. He wasn't fishing for compliments by showing me the film—all the more reason to pay them. I made a mental note to remark on the tonal contrast between the whiteness of the bride, her dress, and the limestone road; and the blackness of the coffin and the trees. It was a pretty deep work of art, though ultimately a failure at capturing Rochelle's essence, which perhaps I alone had glimpsed during the storm on Lac du Bois. My song, if I ever wrote it, would outdo his film. Recently it had occurred to me to repurpose a line from Bob Dylan, "I can't see my reflection in the water," from *Greatest Hits Volume 2*.

Maybe it would have been smart to invite Jason along for this mission. He was a few stages more advanced than Doron on the evolutionary scale. He would know what to do if there was trouble with Hanekamp, if the car broke down, or anything like that. More than me or a stoned foreign voluptuary.

Did I have anything substantial to report to Hanekamp? Would it make any sense to suggest checking whether any hotel registries between here and Los Angeles had been signed with the name Rochelle La Vraie? Was the Pirsig a clue? Was there a point in bringing up dubious claims about the waterski instructor or Kyle Lombardi?

Footsteps distracted me from my deliberation, and the passenger door swung open.

"Hey Eric!"

"Tammy?"

"I thought he told you." What was this curfew-violating, possibly intoxicated camper doing in the back of my borrowed car? Before I could formulate the question, Doron came along and dragged her into the backseat with him. "Good evening, chauffeur. Please take me and my wife here to Yon Yonson's."

I put the car into drive. No other response came to mind that would extricate me from the predicament. Not only did I have to produce some actionable piece of evidence for Hanekamp, I owed Trina an account of my fictitious trip to Menomonee Falls. The immediate challenge was navigating to a bar I'd never visited. In a car I'd never driven. In the dark. While God knows what was happening in the back seat.

"Close your eyes and put your feet in my lap."

"First tell me what you're going to do."

"You have to trust me, Tammy. I would never hurt you."

It wasn't that big a town. I knew Yon Yonson's was somewhere beyond the Stockyard and focused on the road while striving to ignore the backseat exploits of Christopher Clitoris. "What is that?" Tammy's voice was already an octave higher than usual.

"I'm just trying to slip off your sandals. You should get Tevas. They're easy to take on and off and they feel great."

"But they make your feet look like a goat's. What's in the bag?"

"Eyes closed!"

I switched on the air conditioning and turned the stereo up. Rochelle Strauss had been gone for more than forty-eight hours, so according to Hanekamp her life was already in danger. I may have lacked much *mental or moral strength to venture, persevere, and withstand danger, fear, or difficulty,* but it went against my nature to let her slip away without doing at least trying to do something about it.

Unable to resist any longer, I peered into the rear view to see what Doron was up to. He appeared to be slowly rolling a sesame bagel back and forth along the instep of Tammy's foot, then tenderly pressing it into the hollows on either side of her Achilles tendon. Arrhythmic gasps could be heard above the stereo, impairing my ability to stay in my lane. Curiously, I could also hear Tammy chewing gum and occasionally popping bubbles.

Rather than the expected crusty structure with a few letters burned out of its high neon sign, Yon Yonson's turned out to be set in the middle of a recently built strip mall, flanked by a Christian Science Reading Room and a hair salon called Curly Shirley's. I addressed my passengers without turning around. "You guys stay here."

"What? I want to see Yon Yonson's too!"

"You're underage."

"And you're not?"

"Yeah, but you're *way* underage, and he's under the influence of...." Unable to complete the sentence, I started to climb out of the Gremlin, but Doron called me back, asking me to leave the engine on so they could keep the air going.

Yon Yonson's was thick with cigarette smoke, even though it was nearly empty. It felt like a place where fistfights happen over married women. I already had to use the bathroom but decided to hold it, once I spotted the knobless, duct-tape-repaired door. Two of the three Magnavoxes bracketed to the wall above the bar were tuned to the Brewers game. The other one showed Barbara Walters interviewing Adnan Khashoggi. The volume was off, so a whiskered man in a CAT cap and denim jacket the same shade as his jeans was helpfully explicating the report to a catatonic senior on the adjacent barstool.

"The towelhead is a billionaire from Saudi Arabia. He's got a few dozen wives, a fleet of private jets, and a forest of oil wells all to hisself. The U.S.A. don't talk to Iran and Iran don't talk to us, ay, but he talks to both of us. Remember the Ayatollah? This guy threw a lavish party for the hostages when Reagan finally got them out, with hot air balloon rides and Kenny Rogers flown in special. He golfs with Vice President Bush in Maine *and* he prays with the Ayatollah in Tehran.

"So Khashoggi calls Baba Wawa and tells her he's scrambling one of his jets for her. As in pronto. She doesn't ask where he's flying her or what he wants to discuss. She just drops what she's doing and climbs aboard because a guy like that's got the world by the balls so tight it has to ask permission to change undies, and when he says it's news, he's not shitting her, ay."

Hanekamp entered, ordered two bottles of Old Style from the red-headed bartender who had wished me a *Shavuah Tov*, and waved me to a table. He could see I was absorbed in the lecture at the bar, so he let me continue listening.

"And was he ever not shitting Baba Wawa," continued the CAT cap. "We're talking the news scoop of the decade. Two scoops, just like they say in the Raisin Bran commercial. First, Israel is selling 500 U.S.-made heat-seekers" (grabbing his nuts for good measure) "to Iran for their war against Iraq, ay, even though you and me both know Iran is just as likely to wake up tomorrow and point those same missiles at Tel Aviv."

"Good for them," the old man at the bar commented. He'd had nothing to say up until this point, but the destruction of the largest city in the Jewish homeland evidently roused his interest.

"And the second scoop Khashoggi lays on Baba Wawa comes from all the way on the other side of the globe. It's what's happening with the money from the sale of those missiles. Thanks to Lieutenant Colonel Oliver North of the U.S. Marine Corps, $12,000,000 flows to the Contras in Nicaragua, in direct violation of the Boland Amendment."

"The what?"

"Never mind, it's just our democratically elected government breaking its own laws, ay."

"God damn."

"You got that right. But you know what the worst part is? Guess what we got in exchange for 500 missiles. Just guess. Give up? We got one lousy hostage out of Iran. At least he's a Presbyterian."

"Good people," asserted the old man. "My wife's people are Presbyterian."

"What are you talking about, Dad? They're Methodists."

"Isn't that what I said?"

✡

"Why does everybody hate us?"

Hanekamp winced. "*That's* what you got me out here to talk about?"

"No, but still."

"When I visited your camp that day, I do believe that girl with the ill-fitting bikini top shouted 'goy' at the top of her lungs. My dictionary says the term is sometimes derogatory. Was this perhaps one of those times?"

I refrained from mentioning that the girl in question was waiting—wrong word—in the parking lot, probably draining the fuel tank (or was it the battery?) by blasting the air. Instead I said that Faber was still ensconced in the Lodge. "She hasn't bothered interviewing me yet. Mostly she spends time with the girls, getting information out of them about Rochelle. She takes a lot of notes in this three-ring binder that she carries around everywhere."

"Think you could get me the binder?"

"I doubt it."

"Didn't think so. What the hell does she know about jurisdiction, anyway? How is a missing minor in my county not my jurisdiction?"

"You didn't have to leave," I said. "You're the police."

"She's got the attorneys," he reminded me. "You could stuff cotton balls in your nose and still smell the lawsuit on her."

The Brewers game must have concluded satisfactorily, because a small cheer went up in the bar. I sipped my Old Style and drummed my fingers on the table, trying not to think about my bladder or the Gremlin. If that car died in Yon Yonson's parking lot, it was going to be the longest night in my life. (By the way, was that remark about my nose a Jewish joke?)

"Forget the binder," Hanekamp said. "Forget what Faber's trying to get out of you and focus on what she's keeping from you. What does she know about Rochelle that she doesn't want us to know?"

"Do you know anything about motor scooters?" I asked.

"The state issues us actual motorcycles. Why, you have one you want to sell?"

"No, it's just that I promised someone I could get his fixed, but never mind."

"I went down to Winnetka," Hanekamp said, turning serious. "That's some major lakefront property they got there. And nobody's been in or out of it since Wednesday, according to the security detail I talked to."

"What did you think you were going to find—Rochelle lounging by their pool?"

"I didn't know what I'd find," he shot back. "That's why I went. One thing's for sure. The camp isn't the only one to benefit from Frank Strauss's largesse. That name is suddenly going up on museum and hospital walls all over the city."

"Wealthy people can afford be generous, I guess."

"You'd better get back to camp," he said. "Your friends are waiting in the parking lot."

Failing to recognize this dismissal for the provocation that it was, I grasped for the one clue that might help Hanekamp, even though I wasn't certain of its existence. "There's a care package waiting for Rochelle at camp. It arrived on Friday."

"Are you familiar with the Book of Life?" the detective continued, patting down his crew cut. "Every year, the Jewish United Fund publishes a list of who's donated. They break the names down by ranges of giving—fifteen hundred to four thousand, nine hundred, ninety-nine; five thousand to eleven thousand, nine hundred, ninety-nine, and so on. They call it the Book of Life."

"Is that why you hate us?"

Hanekamp nearly smiled. "Last year, Strauss gave between three and five hundred dollars. He was already a rich man by then. Very rich, just not generous. But this year, he's the top giver in the city, upwards of nine million. Number one with a bullet."

Even before my father had moved out, my mother used to study her copy, searching for new marriage material. Now she pored over it like the Bible. She even took it with us to restaurants and circled names with a red ballpoint while waiting for the food to come. So yes, I was familiar with the Book of Life. I just didn't get what it had to do with Rochelle's disappearance.

"Think you could get me the package?" the detective asked.

"I could try."

"Get me the package," he said. "And I'll fix your scooter."

I drove back with a cuddly Doron and Tammy in the backseat and the windows rolled down. The borrowed Gremlin needed to be aired out, and the wind in my face cleared the second-hand smoke from my mind. A few hundred feet before the camp gate, I pulled over to pee on the side of the road. Doron got out and did the same, only with a much more vigorous stream. And so did Tammy. The sound of heavy splashing on dry leaves was unmistakable and caused us all to crack up uncontrollably.

We threw the stale bagels into the woods and brushed the crumbs and seeds out of the back seat before going to bed.

# LEVITICUS

# PART I

On a chill, overcast Sunday morning that felt like the sun had hit the snooze button, Jason Harris did announcements again, but this time the campers didn't chant anything at him. Tammy and Oliver both skipped breakfast. I pictured them arguing over the previous night's hookup and whether their friendship could survive.

Trina's cabin led morning services, choosing "silence" as the theme. This was a known way of avoiding original meditations, but in this instance the tactic was deployed with taste and meaning. The girls passed out strips of black fabric, which we were instructed to tie on as blindfolds.

Cheryl Gilman made a brief statement of introduction. "For the last few days, all of us have been living and breathing in a state of high alert. One of our friends is missing, and we feel this absence upon our shoulders like a weight. The alertness we feel has left us in a seemingly permanent state of fatigue, right down to the marrow. Let us now try to put ourselves in another state, alert not to the dangers beyond but to the mystery within. You don't need Hebrew prayers to worship God. You don't need words at all."

For the silent service, we were allowed to fan out across the grounds. Exiting the chapel and the associations that Kyle had implanted came as a relief. In a stand of diseased elms, I tried to do as Cheryl said, after first replaying in my mind the hesitant, tentative romance that she and I had undertaken the previous summer. Necking in the gazebo, stopping to look at the stars. If only it could start up again, we'd be a much better fit now. Her words were so wise and tender. A gymnast—with not a single ounce of fat on that body.

But anyway, silence.

What did it mean that Frank Strauss had recently become philanthropic? How did this fact fit in with his daughter's disappearance? Detective Hanekamp's investigations, as thorough as they were, led only in circles. On the insides of my eyelids I could picture myself winning glory for finding the girl but couldn't even picture myself doing whatever what was necessary to accomplish that feat. The mystery of Rochelle was infinitely more compelling than the one within my own shriveled consciousness.

> *You swam to me*
> *And not away*
> *You gripped my wrist*
> *That stormy day*

My pathetic attempt at silent meditation died a merciful death thanks to a tap on the shoulder. Siggy VanderBeek stood over me apologetically and handed me a folded piece of paper. Inside were three words:

*See me—Mick*

✡

Mick's office was a prefab structure covered in red siding. As I entered the foyer, G'veret Greenbaum, the eternal camp administrator, lowered her eyes and asked if I had any last words.

Mick beckoned me into his private sanctum and asked me to sit down.

Ms. Faber stood above us, hands behind her back, marionette face in shadows. Throughout the tirade, all the offenses that had *escaped* his notice raced around my mind. Providing livery service to abet a forbidden counselor-camper liaison. (With a vehicle obtained through false pretenses.) Failing to report the party responsible for the malicious destruction of camp property. Photocopying with the intention of committing blackmail. Ideological infractions couldn't have been further from my mind.

The room had two windows, one was stuffed with a giant air conditioning unit, switched off on this chilly morning, and the other was thrown open but obscured by an overgrown shrub. The black leather motorcycle jumpsuit from Mick's office in Skokie was on display here, too, but alongside it hung framed photos and memorabilia—a map of Israel made of flattened mini cereal boxes, a canoe paddle signed by a celebrity Holocaust survivor, a Chicago White Sox banner with the team name transliterated into Hebrew characters.

"You're probably racking your brain right now, trying to remember just what it is you've done," he began, channeling his inner Clint. "I'll get right to the point. You have irreparably desecrated and forever compromised an institution of Jewish learning. That's all. An institution whose credibility has taken twenty-five years to establish. You have singlehandedly betrayed the trust of each and every parent who sends children here with the expectation that they will be safe from a scurrilous propaganda assault."

"This may not be widely known," Faber said, her cartoonish voice struggling to sound somber notes, "but I'm here on behalf of Mr. Franklin Strauss—Rochelle's father and a major new benefactor of the camp. His donation is targeted toward building the future of Jewish leadership in our country. This is an important summer for you, Eric. You can decide to join that future, or you can opt for permanent exile. It's really that simple." When she grinned she resembled an otter or some other mammal that moves easily through the water. Her presence signaled her agreement with Mick, but it also seemed to be assessing the quality of his reprimand, which may have influenced the decidedly personal tact it would soon take.

"Are you with us, Eric? Or are you with the terrorists?"

Faber added, "Although at the moment, Frank Strauss is, like the rest of us, concerned exclusively with Rochelle's whereabouts, in normal circumstances he would definitely want to hear about this. He takes his investment in Jewish leadership very seriously. His generosity is geared to bring the best of the best to our community. It underwrites the plane tickets and stipend for positive role models like Doron Ba'al Shem Tov."

"You were always so considerate and spirited as a camper, Eric," Mick resumed. "You did your part in the cabin and *limudim*. Maybe you were weak on the soccer field. Maybe you weren't the most popular boy, but you made the most of what you had."

I thanked him and immediately wished I hadn't.

"Did something happen to you during the school year?" Mick asked. "Something in your personal life that soured you on your heritage? Because I'm looking at you and feeling like, I don't recognize this boy anymore."

In the process of finding a focal point over Mick's shoulder that would simulate eye contact without having to look directly into those enraged eyes, my glance fell on a shoebox-sized object on a shelf, wrapped in butcher paper and bound with red-and-white twine, with only "Loo" from the address visible. There was yet another infraction unremarked by Mick, this one a felony: conspiring to steal a package entrusted to the camp by the U.S. Postal Service. A warmth suffused my face that must have manifest itself as a smile, because Mick's fury flared higher.

"This may be a joke to you, but for the rest of us who honor the sacrifice that gave rise to the Jewish homeland, it's a matter of life and death. Where will you hide, Eric Weintraub, when the jackboots come marching again? Do you think the next wave of Gestapo thugs will overlook your Jewish name? Your Jewish nose? Your tiny, unloved but circumcised penis? Where will you go if not the State of Israel?"

My Jewish face must have looked perplexed enough because he finally withdrew a sheet of paper from his desk drawer and slid it over to me.

> **A Dangerous Occupation**
> Scott MacLeod
> August 16, 1984
> The killings in June in Borg Rahal and Bidias, southern Lebanese villages of scarcely two thousand people each, testify to the continuing troubles of the Israeli military occupation of southern Lebanon that began two summers ago.
> \*
> For Israel, the irony is that the prolonged occupation—while Israeli politicians and generals work out their latest "Lebanon Solution" to keep away Palestinians and safeguard their northern border—is creating a new enemy.
> \*
> The Red Cross has raised questions about the possible violation of the Fourth Geneva Convention.
> \*
> If the villagers did not have arms, was it necessary to open fire? I asked.
> \*
> "Now people look at us as invaders, not liberators."
> \*
> Then to make sure I understood who he considered was the real enemy, he went on, "Israel is like a snake in Lebanon, Imam Khomeini said that."

It was evidently my turn to respond. The accusation of spreading anti-Israel, probably anti-Semitic propaganda to impressionable American Jewish youth had caught me by surprise. The words on the sheet before me barely corresponded to my recollection of the *limudim* session under the willow, but my character had been indicted, and this was a kind of trial. Above all, I wanted that package. Perhaps the clarity of the objective overrode the confusion of the proceeding.

"I need to call my mom," I said, not having to fake the tears because they were real. Mick and Faber obligingly cleared out of the office, but they were probably standing right outside the door, so I had to pick up the receiver and dial. I didn't necessarily have to call home, but that's what I did. The device on the kitchen counter of my home engaged the microcassette with the outgoing message prerecorded by Panasonic and then switched over to the blank microcassette that received incoming messages. "Hi, Mom, it's me. No emergencies here, just saying hi from camp…. Hi!… Everything's really good here. The big Talent Show is tonight. My co-counselor is a real Israeli named Doron, and I'm learning so much from him about leadership and Israel and all that stuff."

Unconsciously I was tugging at something around my neck, and looking down I realized it was the black strip of fabric that Cheryl's cabin had distributed at services. An impulse took hold of me and was put into effect without any pause for deliberation, all while I kept talking to the answering machine, which my mother never had figured out how to operate.

"It's all coming together this summer, Mom. Being a counselor is different from being a camper, and in a way the counselor experience is helping me make sense of the camper experience from all those previous summers. I'm feeling ready for college, ready to start taking responsibility for my actions and for the world around me. Not that I'm not scared—I am, definitely. But I'm ready, Mom, and I just wanted you to know that."

Throughout this monologue, my cheekbone and shoulder gripped the phone while my fingers tied one end of the blindfold to the twine holding together the shoebox-sized package, which was addressed to Rochelle as suspected. Gingerly I lowered it out the window and into the densest part of the shrub.

My interrogators returned with Rabbi Y'raeh and informed me that he would be sitting in on my Hebrew and *limudim* sessions for the rest of the session. "We are going to study together, Elvis Presley," the elder—and real—rabbi smiled. "We will learn from each other. Maybe some day you will become a great teacher. Independent thought and even outright revolt may even signify vast potential. It is only through considered rebellion that our people change and grow with time."

"I appreciate that, Rabbi."

"Then again," Y'Raeh shrugged, "he could be an insolent little schmuck."

This was hardly a welcome development, but as a punishment it was much lighter than the reprimand had led me to expect. I thanked them and slipped out the door, deciding to return later for the package.

# PART II

Trina and I rehearsed our song in a *kita,* trying out different harmonies, but my mind was elsewhere. The guitar felt wrong in my hands, as though it had somehow increased in size by three percent. Her improvised *ooh*s and *aah*s threw me off tempo, and occasionally I'd stop strumming mid-song and stare into the wall.

"What could Oliver and Tammy be doing in the other *kita*?" I asked.

"The mind reels."

"But they're not an item, right?"

"To the best of my knowledge," she said, "they are not itemizing. That may not even be physically possible in the known universe. Since when are you so interested in the campers' love lives?"

"I'm just not feeling very James Taylor," I said. "How about 'Mony Mony'? Doron would go wild." Pounding out the get-laid-get-fucked riff made the guitar feel like the right size again.

Trina stayed my strumming hand. "How about 'Cat's in the Cradle' or 'The Boxer'?"

"No," I insisted. "I want to play something that Mick would *hate*."

This earned me a blank look that could have been meant to send any number of messages. She could have been reassuring me about my infraction against the Zionist thought police or, alternatively, she could have been censuring me for the same infraction. Her political slant had never previously crossed my mind. (Neither had my own, much.) The look could have been inquiring about the visit with my possibly seriously distressed mother. Maybe she saw through that bogus story and was silently demanding where I got the nerve to drive Doron and Tammy around town in her Gremlin.

Maybe Trina knew something about Rochelle or was trying to guess if I had learned something. Maybe it was a look of love. Maybe she was sick of me. All I got out of that blank look was pure blankness, and anyway, I was preoccupied by the disappearance of Rochelle's package, which someone had removed by the time I had returned to the shrub outside Mick's office.

What did Hanekamp want with the package, anyway? Was it the contents of the box he wanted, or was this a test of my derring-do that he would call upon for a mission of further import?

I had returned three times, tracing my steps back from the stand of elms, even though the package hadn't been with me at services. I had measured the steps between the office and dining hall (it was then that I had spotted Oliver and Tammy), arousing the suspicions of the kitchen staff, which I allayed by claiming to be hungry; I was given a stale egg-flavored bagel.

Neither Mick nor Faber could have found the package. Rabbi Y'raeh had remained, and all three were still engrossed in conversation whenever I'd passed by, not pausing to remark on me crawling around the trunk of the shrub.

I wondered what it would be like having Y'raeh in all my classes. He was an awesome figure, the closest thing we had to an authentic Biblical personage. Maybe his presence would turn me into a super-Jew myself, set me on the path to the rabbinate. Just because I lacked any spiritual feeling didn't mean it wasn't possible to acquire some. Maybe Y'raeh would unleash a hitherto unknown spirituality. Maybe it would help my songwriting or the way girls saw me.

The *kita* trembled with the silence between Trina and me. Finally, our lips met. Whether or not God existed was far from clear, but one fact was beyond dispute: when He put a guitar in my hands, my sexual gravity intensified. That's how Paul Simon won over Princess Leia. The kiss cleared my head of distraction and restored my musical focus. We resumed "Mockingbird" and found a prancing little groove to call our own.

Then we kissed some more, this time with heavy breathing and hands exploring elastic. She told me I was very talented, emboldening me to lower her down onto a bench while I sank to the floor. I untied one of her Reeboks, slid it off, and carelessly tossed it aside. "Eric, what are you doing?" she asked, the excitement in her voice tinged with apprehension.

Without answering I peeled off one red tasseled sock, revealing a small but shapeless foot, like a toddler's drawing. Before Trina could stand, I gripped her ankle, feeling the sock striations on my fingertips, and reached for the bagel the kitchen staff had given me. It was a challenge to brush it along her naked instep as I had seen Doron doing to Tammy, because she kept pulling away. (Interestingly, Hebrew has no word for "foot." They just call it the end of the leg.) I sort of dabbed the bagel in the general vicinity of the sole. Maybe the more varied tactile quality of sesame bagels was the secret. Or maybe my technique fell short.

"Eric? Can I have my foot back, please? I need it to walk out that door."

✡

The grass behind the lodge was cut low. The overgrowth that Oliver and I had traversed Friday night was now landscaped, so I should have known someone had gone over the terrain carefully. Nevertheless, I persisted in believing that if I stomped around long enough, guitar case bumping against my leg and all, eventually I'd come across a fender or a rear-view mirror. My gaze kept seizing on shiny red metal that wasn't there.

So, not only was the package that was addressed to the missing person now itself missing, but the pieces of Rabbi Mick's scooter were gone too. A violent inner shudder gripped me as I began to doubt the existence of the ground I stomped on, the veracity of events that had seemingly happened.

In just over an hour, the curtain would go up on the Talent Show. Heading toward the cabin to get ready, I spotted Jason and a soldier in the chapel. Jason was pointing a movie camera at the soldier, who was positioned in front of a billowing Israeli flag. As I got closer, the soldier turned into Doron, wearing his Israeli Defense Force uniform and balancing a soccer ball on his knee. If it had been possible to obtain a falafel sandwich, he would have been holding it in the other hand. He was reading from a large placard:

*I'm a proud member of Israel's Nahal Brigade, where we uphold* Hayitaron ha-Enoshi—*the human advantage. That's what Paley Lithwick Strauss has, too. As a counselor, it's my honor and privilege to develop a personal relationship with these young people, because I find that when I give them my all, they give it right back to me. That's just an incredible feeling.*

"Excellent," said Jason. "Now say it again but slower, and with more of a Sephardic tinge."

Doron swigged some water and recited his lines again. Then he beckoned me over. "Eric, you should be in Jason's movie too," he said. "Jason, you've got to put Eric in. He could play for you!"

I opened my case and pulled out the guitar. "This for the promotional movie?" I asked, busting out the latest version of the Rochelle song, without disclosing the inspiration.

> *Am I swimming, or am I drowning?*
> *Are we rising, or sinking down?*
> *The strangest sense that I've ever felt before.*
> *Like stepping through an invisible door.*

"Yeah," Jason said. "My dad's suddenly gotten very gung-ho about this." He reached for the water that Doron had been drinking from, which I realized wasn't water.

"Maybe Faber said something," I offered, pretending not to mind that he had cut me off.

Doron simulated a carnal act with the soccer ball. "Do you think Rochelle's dad is fucking her?"

"Fucking his own daughter?"

"No, I mean the replicant."

"I seriously doubt it."

"Too bad. She must be some kind of specially designed fucking machine, I bet."

Ignoring this, I shared a theory with Jason that had been growing like a tumor on the edge of my consciousness. "You know how you said last night that the camp was in some kind of money trouble?"

"Sure as shit. His insurance premium alone has tripled in the past five years. The rates go up every time a poor soul chokes or strokes at some other camp in Buttfuck, North Dakota."

"Exactly. And you know how Frank Strauss gets rich by taking over companies that are about to go out of business?"

"How the hell is that supposed to work?" Jason threw his head back and gargled the clear liquid from Doron's canteen.

"I don't know. It's some kind of voodoo economics thing, or whatever."

"I'm listening."

"Well, could the camp be, like, his next takeover target? Maybe he just donated all that money and joined the board of directors so he could sell it all out."

"Or maybe none of that would have even crossed his mind, but now that we lost his daughter he might be giving it some serious consideration. This whole place could be a golf resort before you know it."

"A casino. They're giving away gambling licenses to Indian reservations these days."

"What makes Indians so special?" asked Doron.

"We fucked them over pretty royally—remember?"

"Speak for yourself. What did I ever do to the Indians? Jews got fucked over pretty royally, too—remember?"

It was always easiest to ignore Doron. "What if they built a multiplex? Imagine Rochelle La Vraie's face, twenty feet tall."

Jason's crooked smile fell limp. "This could be the very last summer of camp."

"Tonight could be the very last Talent Show," I added.

"Tonight could be my very last chance to fool around with Cheryl Gilman," Doron said, suddenly catching our sense of despair.

"Hey kids," Jason grimaced. "Let's put on a show."

# PART III

Afternoon shaded into to evening as one hundred and fifty campers took their seats on metal risers and on a tarp covering the damp grass. Jason served as master of ceremonies, leading each of five units in their fight songs to warm up for the annual Talent Show. Unless you knew, you couldn't tell that he was drunk.

"We've got a *really big* show lined up for you tonight. It's so amazing, so *wildly unbelievable,* that Paley Lithwick Strauss may never be the same again. Kicking off this *blistering explosion* of homegrown camp talent is a trio that goes by the name Men Without Yarmulkes!"

*Em-em-em-em*
*Ay-ay-ay-ay*
*Tee-tee-tee-tee*
*Zee-zee-zee-zee*
*Ay-ay-ay-ay*
*Matza*
*BALL!*

The premiere act was followed by a pretty-darn-good breakdancing demonstration, a rafters-shaking rendition of "God Bless America," and an 11-year-old Madonna impersonator complete with bared midriff.

Jason paced back and forth, holding his head in his hands. "That was truly... I don't know what to say about that, Shira, because anything I would say could and would be held against me in a court of law. So! Ladies and gentlemen, campers and counselors, rabbis, special guests, and...Dad! Our next act is a skit from three boys from Doron and Eric's cabin. They describe it as Saturday Night Live meets the Nuremberg Trials. I'm not even going to guess what that's supposed to mean. I'm just going to stand facing the wall and hope it doesn't last too long."

Max, Andrew, and Kyle got up on stage. Max's blackface and shades signified Stevie Wonder. "I'd like to say 'thank you' tonight to all you *beautiful* people," he grinned, spastically rolling his head toward the painted backdrop. A tracksuit and headband turned Kyle into Richard Simmons, who pranced around lisping "Thith ith thooo thpecial!" Initially it wasn't clear who Max was supposed to be—a mailman?—but once he opened his mouth I realized it was *The Honeymooners'* Jackie Gleason playing Ralph Kramden as popularized by Eddie Murphy.

"Richie boy!" he bellowed. "C'mere Richie boy, there's something I've been meaning to tell you. You know what I want to do to you, and I know that you know what I want to do to you."

"Help me *thtretch* my quads?" squealed Richard Simmons.

"And you know that I know that you know what I want to do to you!" He proceeded to mount the exercise guru, imitating Eddie Murphy's imitation of Ralph Kramden's *hummuna-hummuna-hummuna-hummuna* and eliciting hysterics from the audience.

Stevie Wonder groped his way across the stage, crooning "I Just Called to Say I Love You" off-key, and soon he was bumping into, and more or less humping, Ralph and Richie.

The laughter gained magnitude with each thrust and blind pratfall as Ralph, Richie, and Stevie formed what was commonly known as a *boof train* and were chug-chug-chugging in a tiny circle when Rabbi Mick clambered onstage and spread his arms wide, hands facing out, fingers splayed.

The audience fell silent, and the boys hung their heads, suppressing smiles. "I'm afraid that the 'act' you just saw is inappropriate for our institution of Jewish learning," Mick said. "It failed to rise to the level of satire, and I hope that the perpetrators—and their counselors—deeply regret that you had to be subjected to their offensive behavior."

After that, Jason took his time reinflating the mood before bringing on Trina and me. "We're *making history* tonight. Not just because our next act is here to *deliver us from evil*. Not just because they are *guaranteed to anoint us* with sweet musical blessings unlike anything we have ever experienced in this arena." Scattered catcalls and hoots rose in response. "Not just because these two *nuclear power plants* of musical talent have never *melted down* together on our stage before. Not just because—well, besides being two *immensely caring* and spirited counselors who make *each and every day* in each and every camper's life *richer and sweeter*—not just because we love them. It's also a treat for all of us tonight because one of them is in for a *big surprise*."

Before I saw, I knew. The realization came down like a mudslide. A middle-aged woman in a white mink and oversize sunglasses, weirdly similar to those worn by Max as Stevie Wonder, toddled through the crowd to the stage.

Mom.

The message I had left on her machine had mentioned the Talent Show, but it was never intended as an invitation.

Mom?

She'd tried in the past to show an interest in my songwriting but couldn't seem to help comparing me to Neil Diamond.

"Hi Mom!" I mouthed.

"Let's extend a warm fuzzy Paley Lithwick Strauss welcome to Eric Weintraub's *mother!*" Jason trilled.

There was nothing to do but play the damn song. Trina and I entered from opposite sides, converging on a microphone stand at center stage. She moved like her joints were springs, and her voice acquired a bluesier shade than it had had in rehearsal, giving every line a licentious undercurrent. Somehow this rising Brandeis sophomore managed to channel Tina Turner instead of Carly Simon.

> *Everybody have you heard*
> *He's gonna buy me a mockingbird*
> *And if that mockingbird don't sing*
> *He's gonna buy me a diamond ring*
> *And if that diamond ring won't shine*
> *He's gonna surely break this heart of mine*

I tried to keep pace by swamping up the chords, but Trina-slash-Tina ruled the roost. She swung her hips and shimmied her shoulders while I launched a furiously strummed solo, and before I could prevent her she had knelt down and extended a hand to bring my mom onstage with us. The three of us danced around in circles, and the applause crested.

"We're a big hit, Eric!" Mom declared. "We're famous!"

And then everyone was on their feet and I realized they weren't applauding *us* anymore. A pickup truck was rolling up the road behind us, towing a shiny speedboat emblazoned with the name *The Golden Calf*. Behind the wheel: the Rick Springfield lookalike who'd given the camp a day of water-skiing. And standing in the payload: Rochelle and a beaming older man— Frank Strauss, I presumed—in a purple-checked shirt buttoned to the top.

Before this spectacle had time to settle in, the speakers roared to life with a familiar pulsating rhythm. Trina, Mom, and I backed away to make room for an unscheduled performer.

> *I know what boys like*

*I know what guys want*
*I know what boys like*
*I've got what boys like*

A mysterious figure on a two-wheeled vehicle climbed the ramp to take the stage. The vehicle, a reincarnation of Mick's Vespa, had sprouted chrome in every imaginable place, and while its body was still red, it was a *redder* red, glowing hot from within.

It was easier to describe the rider's costume than to identify who it was. A wavy red wig and distressed fishnet stockings were set off by matching black leather vest, short shorts, and high boots still redolent of the tannery. Streaks of eye shadow and slashes of red lipstick at once accentuated and obscured the face of the rider.

*I make them want me*
*I like to tease them*
*They want to touch me*
*I never let them*

Oliver Berkowitz, aka Olivia Neutron Bomb, skidded to a halt at the foot of the stage, dismounted, and gyrated with practiced abandon. Rabbi Mick stood still as a Han Solo in carbonite.

# PART IV

Rochelle was missing again the next day. All the girls in her cabin said she had fallen asleep in her bunk, and two even swore they had seen her brushing her teeth early in the morning, but she never made it to breakfast. Oliver didn't show up, either, but his absence had an easy explanation. A fourteen-year-old boy who had just shaken his moneymaker in leather short shorts could hardly expect a hero's welcome. After the Talent Show he had elected to sleep in the Lodge and was probably enjoying his waffles and hash browns away from the scorn of his peers. In the commotion after the performance, I had nabbed him for a fractured exchange.

"Nice bike!"

"Thanks, I had a little help."

"I was going to ask someone, but by the time I got there, it—"

"Siggy."

"Siggy! Of course, I was thinking Hanekamp, the cop."

"You got your goy, I got mine," he'd shrugged, face still smeared with makeup. "And by the way, thanks for all this."

"What do you mean?"

"That was your arm, wasn't it?"

"*What* was my arm?"

"Sticking out of Mick's office window? Lowering the package down?" I'd nodded like I had caught on. "It's real hair, not acrylic. But you won't find this shade of red in nature."

"It's like plastic roses at sunset," I'd said, delighting him with the simile.

"But let me tell Doron myself how much *he* inspired me. Well, him and Rabbi Mick both. You know those tapes he tried to ruin with his farts?"

"Yeah?"

"And you know that Rabbi Mick story about the simpleton who repairs the flaw in the precious sapphire?"

"Of course, but…"

"Think of the farts on those tapes as the flaw in the gem. I couldn't delete them so I embellished them. Just as the simpleton incorporated his crack into an overall floral design, I incorporated mine into part of an immersive *vroom vroom* performance. The rev of the engine makes the whole costume."

"I'm going to welcome Rochelle back," I'd said. But first I'd had to deal with my mother, who'd been shadowing Frank Strauss with the zeal of a disciple. The light had reflected more cleanly off his cheekbones so that he'd seemed to be outlined in pure gold. His crisp purple-checked shirt had made her off-white mink look drab.

"Did you see my son play guitar?" she'd asked him.

"No, Mom," I'd broken in. "They pulled up at the very end of our number."

"Your son is very talented," Strauss had assured her. "If he ever wants lessons, the best jazz guitarist in Chicago is a personal friend." Even though jazz guitar nauseated me, the offer, coming from him, sounded enticing.

"He gets it from me," she'd fibbed, eyeing him like she wanted to spread cream cheese on him and have him for brunch.

"Thanks for coming, Mom," I'd said. "But you'd better get going if you want to make it home before midnight."

Mick had arrived at that moment to pronounce my suggestion "nonsense," with a grand sweep of the arm. "The mother of 'the last one to see Rochelle alive' is a guest of the camp tonight. We'll have a room made up for her in the Lodge."

This cavalier attitude toward the missing-person drama that had gripped the whole camp—not just me, right?—had stuck in my craw. Was it naïve to have imagined that something terrible could have happened to her? Was it just a desperate hope for something dramatic to happen in my ordinary life that drove me into the arms of the Wisconsin State Police?

What I thought was courage may have actually been an outlet for adolescent energy. What I thought was tragic was actually comic. The joke was on me all along.

Obviously, being on staff didn't qualify me for the adult world, where a different set of rules applied to the very wealthy. The rich guy could whisk his daughter off to the Milwaukee Air and Water Show without so much as mentioning it to her counselor, sending the whole place into a tizzy.

Prayers were muttered. Authorities were alerted. But the camp got this gleaming new speedboat out of it, so what's the harm?

"Birthday buddy!" The tight squeeze she gave me hurt, well, it hurt so good. My rancor immediately had evaporated when confronted with the soft ivory of Rochelle's complexion, the luminescence of those cobalt eyes. Part of me was back on Lac du Bois, buffeted by sheets of rain, watching the water bead on that perfect skin.

"Nice boat!" I'd smiled, inwardly realizing my own disappointment in not performing "Rochelle's Song" at her memorial service.

"We definitely have to get you up on skis tomorrow," she'd said. "I actually think it would be really good for you. Any worries you have, they just get left behind in the spray." She knew as well as I did that it would never happen. Whether it was posture, balance, courage, or some combination of the three, the stuff it took to water ski was just missing. I would never outrace my worries. The visibility of my worries further aggravated the predicament. The people I wanted to impress would simply never be impressed.

"It was so cool of your dad to buy that boat for the camp."

A shadow had flitted over her eyes as she'd deadpanned, "Yeah, he's way cool."

✡

Wearing pressed jeans and an oversized Choose Jews T-shirt, Oliver bounced down from the Lodge alongside my mom. God knows what they had found to talk about, and how much of it concerned me, but they had obviously hit it off.

"I'm so glad you two met," I said, attempting a tone that couldn't be accused of either sarcasm or sincerity. "This wasn't quite a typical day at camp, Mom, but it's great that you got to see it for yourself. I know you need to get back, though."

"Nonsense," said Oliver, who had mastered a precise impersonation of Mick. "The mother of 'the last one to see Rochelle alive' must spend a few *days* here, at least."

When I told them Rochelle hadn't shown up for breakfast, they noted that she wasn't with her father either. Frank Strauss was still at the Lodge, lounging around with Rabbi Mick and the Rick Springfield guy who'd delivered the boat—whose name turned out to be Serge.

"Something about him gives me a weird feeling," I said.

"He's very sweet," my mom insisted. "Maybe you just aren't used to Brazilians."

"He's most certainly Brazilian," Oliver added, with an undertone of naughtiness I couldn't decode. "If he were any more Brazilian, he'd be *Brazil*."

"Oliver," I asked, "Did Rochelle say anything to you about what happened in Milwaukee?"

"Did you check the waterfront?" my mom said. "She probably couldn't wait to get out on the lake with that yacht."

"That makes sense," I said, determined not to panic about Rochelle again. Anyway, I had to get ready for my first Hebrew class overseen by Rabbi Y'raeh. He had promised to meet under the willow at noon.

# PART V

The second time around, Rochelle's absence weighed less than a feather on our shoulders. We were determined to enjoy ourselves regardless, and our determination made us lose our minds a bit.

Giddy Yids. Heebs with the heebie-jeebies.

Nobody canceled Hebrew and *limudim*, but nobody called for them, either. Frank and Serge departed in the pickup, and most of Monday went for waterskiing courtesy of The Golden Calf, an impromptu soccer tournament organized by Doron, and an epic squirt gun battle. Shooting the film reel for Jason seemed to have rekindled his inner *sabra*. Apparently he'd decided to show these weak and depraved Americans some Zionist fury.

"Kick through the ball, Rambo!" he growled at Kyle, who scurried after an errant pass. "If you spent half the time on sport that you spend on moussing your pubes, you might be less of an embarrassment." When Andrew caught a penalty kick in the nuts and lay fetal in the grass, Doron said it didn't matter, he hadn't been using his nuts much anyway. He squirted the boy execution-style in the temple with a toy uzi and ordered the game to proceed.

My mother hadn't said good-bye, so it seemed reasonable to assume she could be found somewhere on campus. She wasn't watching soccer and had never been up on water skis. Without exactly going in search of her, I roamed past the girls' cabins and back along the limestone path toward the Lodge. Of course I was also keeping my eyes peeled for clues to Rochelle's whereabouts, even though it was by no means clear how to recognize one. Would a hotel registry or bullet casing appear in my path?

An aluminum Louisville Slugger—31 inch, 30 ounce, if I was not mistaken—had been discarded on the side of the path, but there were no obvious bloodstains on it.

My mother's Caprice Classic was still parked in the lot. The coating of limestone dust made the two beiges of its exterior almost identical. Clothing jumbled inside along with hair care products and cosmetics. She liked to be prepared for any social occasion that might arise. You never knew when the situation might call for turquoise faux-crocodile boots, a nearly matching rhinestone-studded velour sweat suit, and a half can of Aqua Net. The cassette in the player—Barbra Streisand's Guilty—had recently replaced the eight-track tape she'd bought five years before.

She had said that a *machon* summer would be good for me. Now I wondered if my absence for ten weeks might have been good for her, too. Soon I would be off in DeKalb, anyhow, but it was apparent, if fuzzily so, that she couldn't have the house to herself soon enough. At camp we always talked about what we missed back home—TV, soft beds, real food—maybe we even confessed to missing our parents. But thoughts of what our parents did without us never crossed our minds. Surveying this backseat assortment awoke me to this new dimension.

Beside the Caprice Classic was the Jaguar that had brought Ms. Faber. While the XJ6 had been pristine upon arrival, countless scuffs and scratches now covered its Brunswick green shell, as though it had been assaulted, somewhat weakly, with an aluminum bludgeon. The leaping-cat hood ornament had endured a particularly vicious beating; repeated strokes had knocked it downward and off center.

To me, the Jaguar's sunroof epitomized the good life, which unmistakably meant the financial good life, not just freedom from worry about the MasterCard bill but a certain kind of American authority that was all around me but well out of reach. A convertible was flashy and impractical, but the ability to open a rectangle of fresh air above you at the push of a button, that separated gods from men.

I wiped aside a layer of dust and peered inside. In this back seat was a lidless 9 West shoebox holding three incongruous objects: a glossy magazine creased lengthwise, a roll of silver duct tape, and what I thought then was an orange pistol. Orange like a traffic cone. It wasn't a toy, but it wasn't a weapon, either. It was for shooting flares in case of a road emergency.

Just as that Mae-West-by-way-of-suburban-Atlanta voice reached my ears, I noticed Faber crouched below the payphone. I tried to get close enough to overhear without my footsteps on the limestone giving away my presence. To accommodate the crouch, her skirt was hiked up high enough on her toned thighs that black panties were visible.

"I'm going to, Mama. I swear this time I'm going to. I'm going to sit him down and say, 'Do you even consider the effect your actions have on other people? Such as me, for instance. Such as your wife and daughter?' Exactly! 'The people who are most loyal to you in this world—those are the ones you choose to injure? You do know that what you do is both twisted and cruel, right.' I know he will, but that's not what I want. I am not looking for another bonus or another raise, thank you. I know he will, Mama. Believe me, nobody knows this man like I do."

"I could write a book," she continued. "And maybe I will. the *Sun-Times* could publish chapter one. 'Multi-millionaire's Personal Assistant Tells All'." A polytonal groan stretched out over the next five seconds. "All all all all all all, yes, I mean all, Mama! Every single midnight phone call I got, every 'Hello, Vicki, dear, I'm on the payphone at Ohio and St. Clair, and my wallet seems to be empty. Could you pick me up, please, dear?' Every loan to a 'friend' and every 'We don't have to tell anybody about this, Vicki'."

I wouldn't have guessed her name was Vicki. That changed everything. It reduced "Ms. Faber" to an alumna who sat on the board of her old sorority, the go-to last-minute babysitter for her sister's kids. Suddenly I could picture her on the kitchen floor of a high-rise condominium, polishing a pair of worn of heels. I could see a freezer packed with Lean Cuisine and Häagen-Dazs.

"Mama!" she laughed. "I don't even know. It's his poor little rich daughter's overnight camp in Wisconsin somewhere. Moconomowee or Mowocona-something. No, I don't think he wants to wear my shoes. We do have the same taste in men, though."

The clear, dry sunshine made the skin under my arms tacky. Only a long shower and a close shave would restore me to a state of readiness for the task, as-yet-undisclosed, that something told me lay ahead. I brought Oliver's boombox into Noah's Ark and turned up the volume on *Bookends*.

> *Hang onto your hopes my friend*
> *That's an easy thing to say*
> *But if your hopes should pass away*
> *Simply pretend*
> *That you can build them again*

Sulfurous water scalded the roots of my hair, clots of lather smacked against the graffiti-covered shower walls, and time slowed to a crawl. Instead of visualizing the heroic act that destiny held in store for me, my psyche conjured Cheryl Gilman's form emerging from the steam. The joy-buzzer guitar riff of "A Hazy Shade of Winter" somehow embodied her taut gymnast's contours encased in bathing suit material, the airtight fit of nylon snapping to conform to her physique, the red marks that elastic left on her skin.

Aloe-infused shower gel made all my nerve endings clickety-clack in time with the music. The jolt of freezing water that concluded all showers failed to calm the fever, which continued to shoot up and down my spine in the silence that followed.

The silence. The silent prayer service she led. The black blindfold. The fleeting encounter with her pubic region the summer before. It was on a thin towel by the lake, the last night of the session. One set of my fingertips wandering up a thigh, the other down her stomach. Which had first reached the fringe of thicket? And, anyway, what had arrested my progress toward third base? I couldn't remember her pushing my hand away. Had I, then, stopped myself, afraid of revealing my anatomical ignorance?

(If pressed to reveal the extent of my knowledge, which thank God never happened, I would have probably asserted that there was something called the clitoris, located either deep inside the vagina or else up front near the top. The dictionary put it "anterior to the vulva," but that didn't help. I had also heard of something called the G spot. Which either was or wasn't the same thing, and maybe didn't exist. If luck or fate somehow enabled me to locate either of these things, I would have had no more idea what to do with it than I would the insides of a boombox. God is a mystery, but the mystery is not God.)

Or did a misbegotten sense of honor prevent me from crossing the threshold of a serious relationship that wasn't emotionally supportable? Oh, to stand at that crossroads again! Even to humiliate myself!

The intensity of the recollection fogged my vision, and I tripped back to bed, trembling in anticipation of release. The towel around my waist cut off circulation to my nether regions, and yet the engorgement refused to subside. Failing to open the cabin door wide enough, I attempted to slip through sideways. Owing to the tensile strength of the door's spring, it very nearly clamped onto the ache beneath the towel, and in my hasty maneuver to dodge it, the boombox slipped from my damp grip and crashed to the floor. The control for AM radio must have detonated, because Simon and Garfunkel was immediately replaced by a deep Southern voice urging me to accept Jesus deep into my heart. Not right now, thank you. My big toe found the switch to turn off the radio.

I yanked a dress sock from my laundry bag and put it to use while awkwardly draping the towel over my heaving shoulders. Colored spots floated before my eyes as my wildly pulsating imagination zoom-lensed all over Cheryl's body, with the action intermittently interrupted by high-speed footage of Rochelle, her face sprinkled with water and her head thrown back to expose a luscious pair of collarbones. It was as though two girls could squeeze into a single bathing suit and still be two girls.

A clearing throat shoved time back to its accustomed pace and signaled that I had been mistaken to assume solitude. The sound in the throat was not adolescent but rather sexagenarian. A long moment—less than a second, probably—of cognitive dissonance straddled the swimsuit fantasy and the rabbinic reality.

"*Rabeinu shel olam*, master of the universe," intoned Mordechai Y'raeh. "Each of us worships you in our own individual way. Some of us recite beautifully wrought Hebraic verse polished lovingly like an heirloom from generation to generation. Others must confine themselves to inarticulate grunts. Let not the form of the prayer distract you from the sincerity of our plea for your goodness and mercy.

"Not buying it, eh? Well, how about this? Would you believe he's strategically confusing the Evil Impulse by giving in without a struggle?"

The source of the voice was less than ten feet away. I was afraid to turn my head and face the rabbi, which permitted him to continue.

"This is no joke, eh? Okay, *Rabeinu shel olam*, master of the universe, let's have it out. Like you did with Abraham over the destruction of Sodom and Gomorrah. As a special favor to me, please defer smiting this wicked boy for another moment or two. Also, we promise to tear down the smutty picture of the *shikse* in the cowgirl outfit."

"Rabbi," I rasped.

"It is true, the Talmud says, 'Whoever wastes seed, thinks impure thoughts, or does something to cause temptation deserves death.' It is also true that Rav Ami said it is as if he sheds blood. Rav Ashi says it is as if he worships strange deities. Rav Acha bar Yashya said whoever wastes seed equates himself to an animal. Just like an animal does not care what it does, so too this person randomly commits this sin. Just like an animal is set aside to be slaughtered and does not receive life in the future world so to this person stands to die and does not live in the future world."

I uttered the word rabbi more clearly, but he nonetheless continued: "It is not the death of sinners that you seek but that they should turn from their ways and live. Isn't that true? And besides, let's face it. If this rule of yours were uniformly enforced, this camp would be decimated, if not completely depopulated."

"Rabbi Y'raeh, if I could just have a moment to get dressed, I can get ready to start *limudim* with you."

"Good. I'll be right outside." The rabbi's distinctive thump-drag, thump-drag gait reverberated against the cabin walls.

I swore on Misty Norwood's breasts that if nobody found out about this, I would never do it again.

# PART VI

Rochelle had been one of those popular girls who never let anybody get too close. Before her second disappearance, nobody would have recognized Tammy and Oliver as her two best friends at camp. Tammy, with her indefatigable enticement of the male sex, might well have regarded the "beautiful, reckless daughter of a multimillionaire" as a rival, but she also was capable of fierce devotion to the people she cared about, be they campers or staff. Oliver was one of them, and his loyalty to Rochelle had rubbed off on her.

Though perhaps her devotion wasn't completely pure, as I discovered upon finding Tammy and Oliver in the *kita* they had used before the Talent

Show. Jason's camera and tripod stood in the middle of the room. Wearing Oliver's wig from the Talent Show, Tammy was wedged into a small desk, a cosmetics kit arrayed before her, saying "But how exactly is this supposed to rescue the kidnapped JAP?"

"You'll see," Oliver said, as if he had been waiting for me to finally turn up. "Eric, can you give us a ride tonight after lights-out?"

"That doesn't sound like such a smart idea—and not just because that wasn't my car."

"Was she mad about the seeds we spilled?" Tammy asked, and for an instant she seemed to be referring to Rabbi Y'raeh's intervention to keep God from smiting me.

"I think… my driving privileges have been revoked."

"Don't *tell* me!" Oliver cried. "I thought you guys were forever."

"Where do you want to go, anyway?"

"We called your cop friend," Trina explained. "He sounds nice. He said he remembered me."

"What'd you call him for?"

"The same reason you did," Oliver answered. "We all know Rabbi Mick won't do jack shit. For whatever reason, he either can't or won't look for Rochelle. Maybe he's afraid to disturb Frank Strauss. Maybe he can't deal with the bad publicity. Maybe he *wants* Rochelle out of the way. Is that so hard to imagine?"

"Just because she ran off with her dad to buy a speedboat last time," conjectured Tammy. "Doesn't mean she's not in danger this time."

"*If* that's what even happened last time," added Oliver.

"Do you guys know anything about what happened in Milwaukee?" I asked. "Rochelle seemed kind of pissed at her dad."

"That's exactly why we need a ride tonight."

"What did Hanekamp say?" I asked.

"He said we should go back to waterskiing, which means he definitely heard about her return and probably knows she's gone again. Before hanging up he said this was not his jurisdiction—only, sarcastically. But he would listen to you."

"What makes you say that?"

"You're a counselor!"

I gestured at the film equipment. "And this is…?"

"Can we show him?" Tammy asked Oliver. He flipped off the overhead bulb and aimed a spot at her.

"How's my hair?" she asked.

He expertly adjusted the wig and tugged on the front of her top, which resembled surgical scrubs dyed mauve, only nicer, and then took his place behind the camera. "Claire's lipstick, take 6," he called. "In three. 3, 2, 1, action!"

Tammy stared into the middle distance and, in a fluffier voice than her own, said, *"Okay."* She looked downward for a moment. *"You have to swear to God you won't laugh."* Then she shook her head in dismay of her own nerve and uncapped a lipstick. *"I can't believe I'm actually doing this,"* she sighed, before extending the lipstick two twists and inserting it, pointing up, front and center, between brassiere and sternum. Inclining her neck, she gave a practiced shake of the false red locks. Oliver zoomed in as Tammy expertly maneuvered her face into her bosom—which, it dawned on me, was too ample for the scene she was reenacting, and yet the original still eluded me.

But then her head snapped upward, and she flashed a triumphant, half-open, Marilyn-esque smile. The precise shade of her dewy lips, somewhere between peach and apricot, instantly activated my cortical memory. Tammy Berk was Claire Standish, Molly Ringwald's debutante detainee from *The Breakfast Club*, and I found myself applauding her stunt like a smitten Anthony Michael Hall..

"Better," declared Oliver, clearly not satisfied. "But that was still about twenty percent too fast. Think *uphill*, not *downhill*. Claire is riding the lift *up*, not gliding *down*. Give the spectators time to absorb what you're doing. The physical poetry of it, the ballet. It's not a stunt, it's a statement. It's *seduction.*" In the twenty-four hours since Oliver's showstopper, he had already become something of an auteur.

Tammy clicked her tongue and appealed to me. "What did *you* think?"

"It was uncanny," I said. "Don't listen to him."

"Give me that," Oliver barked, helping her off with the wig and blouse and showing more interest in the wardrobe than the body underneath.

Tammy's chest in a bra shouldn't have been that different from Tammy's chest in a bikini top. Yet my libido snapped clumsily to attention in the few seconds it took for her to slip into the Choose Jews shirt and, before putting her arms through the sleeves, wiggle out of the sacred piece of lingerie. Oliver, by contrast, nonchalantly took it from her and strapped it on himself. Having tangled with bra clasps in the past, I marveled at his dexterity. He slipped on the wig and surgical blouse and then folded himself into the desk as she took her place behind the camera.

The instant the word "action" sounded, the *kita* entered another time and place. Oliver's performance as Claire Standish exposed Tammy's for the pale imitation that it was. It wasn't just that he had Claire's flat chest. He fully inhabited the spoiled yet sensitive, fierce yet fragile girl with an authenticity that somehow surpassed the original, imbuing her with a backstory and—dare I say—a *soul* while at the same time skewering her Waspy uptightness. He had even picked a truer shade of lipstick.

"That," I sputtered. "Was phenomenal. But what does it have to do with Rochelle?" Was the red wig a real clue or a red herring?

"Nothing!" shrugged Oliver—as himself again, though he was still wearing Claire Standish's blouse, hair, and lipstick. "And everything. Feel for yourself."

# PART VII

Rabbi Mick made a good show of enjoying the way that Siggy and Oliver had paint-jobbed and souped-up his scooter. He'd zipped himself into his black leather jumpsuit and rode high. Resembling the love object in a Pat Benatar video, he swerved smartly around clusters of campers shuffling between activities. That afternoon he zoomed into the Horseshoe and stomped up our cabin steps, disturbing a rare moment of peace in the daily post-lunch rest period. The boys had already flipped through all available *Sports Illustrated*s and listened to *Born in the U.S.A.* on their Walkmans so many times that its dozen songs would follow them into the afterworld.

The latest rage among Kyle, Max, and Andrew was bullshit, the card game, which trains young minds to tell and recognize lies. The object is to get rid of all your cards. You take turns laying pairs or threes face down, claiming increasingly better hands until one of your opponents calls "bullshit." The claim is then checked—if it turns out to be true, all the discards go into his hand, and if it's false, you take all the discards into yours. The game of bullshit embodied the supreme narrative of the adolescent male—narrative itself, the ability to tell a *convincing* story. If you could bullshit, then it didn't matter if your family was rich or poor.

Kyle held most of the deck. His failings as a liar, as a storyteller, radiated off him like an unwashable stink. Nobody explicitly connected his inability to put over bullshit to his canine fable about Rochelle in the chapel, but that was in the air.

When Mick barged in, Oliver had been reorganizing his cassettes, Doron had been circling items in an Army Navy surplus catalogue, and I had been browsing Marx's *Capital*. One whole shelf of the camp library was taken up with a set of *Cambridge Classics—Aristotle to Zarathustra*. The source of Frank Strauss's fortune continued to plague me, and maybe pondering his wealth through what I flattered myself to be a revolutionary lens would make sense of it—or at least inspire some song lyrics.

Strauss bought from people who underestimated what they had, and he sold to people who overestimated what they wanted. There was nothing inherently valuable about these commodities; the estimates were *metaphysical* propositions. He was some kind of mystic, I concluded.

In spite of Mick's blustery entrance, there was a right-side-only smile on his face we'd never seen before. He hadn't come to reprimand us about anything. In fact, he had brought a pizza, which he offered almost apologetically.

"It isn't hot anymore," he said, "but it's still good," adding "*kosher* pepperoni" with a wink before disappearing.

At first, nobody reacted. It may not have been piping hot, but it was warm enough that soon the smell filled the cabin. Certainly it was still edible. For as long as anyone could remember, pizza cast a powerful spell upon our kind. It was "real" food. Even the counselors, who could in theory scarf it nearly every night at the Stockyard, were unable to resist a slice or two when it appeared on campus.

"What do you think he did to it?" Andrew finally said.

"What do you mean, *did?*" Doron said, though neither he nor anybody else moved to open the box, with its cartoon Italian chef on the lid.

"Like, did he sneeze on it first?"

Remembering the snotty challah, I turned to Oliver, who gave me a *What! I had to sneeze!* look.

"Or jizz on it," Max said.

"Check if he brought one to the other cabin" Doron said. "Maybe we could give it to them."

"And get something for it in return!" added Oliver.

"Yeah," said Max, "Like, 'Hey, can we have your turn with the speed-boat? We'll give you this pizza that Mick jizzed all over.' That might work."

"Pizza's pizza," Andrew summarized. "It's like cigarettes in prison."

"Wait a minute," I said, approaching the box. "We don't even know he jizzed on it. In fact, there would be no reason to even imagine anything like that if Max hadn't said that."

"So are you gonna eat it, then?" Max challenged.

"Not that hungry," I shrugged.

"So what's up with Mick bringing us a pizza?" Kyle asked. "The last time he set foot in this cabin, he was ready to send us all home for Rat Fucking. Now he shows up with a gift for no good reason? And did you see that sick little smile lurking under his mustache? And the way he just slipped out of here? I wouldn't be surprised if the thing wasn't booby-trapped to explode. Whoever opens that box is going to get a face full of shrapnel, probably."

"Remember what Jason did to that pizza he brought to us after lights out last year?" Max said. "We were always whining about how the other cabin had gotten woken up for midnight pizza twice, but he hadn't brought us pizza even once. So he made us a deal. He said, 'Look, as soon as we get through one whole day without even one of you asking for pizza even once, that's the night I'll bring you pizza.' But then day after day, *someone* would say something like, 'Is *tonight* the night you're going to bring us pizza?' and he'd be like, 'Not anymore!' So finally there were like two days left in the session, and he got so sick of us ruining our own pizza chances that he did bring us one, even though somebody *had* asked that afternoon, but first he sprinkled a ton of those red pepper flakes all over it. And he made us eat it in the dark."

From the way Max told the story, it was impossible to tell whether he loathed or admired Jason for what he had done. "That's when I learned what Preparation H is for," he added.

"Two years ago, when I was a camper," I began. "We got a special afternoon in town. It was supposed to be Madison, but the year before, there was a trip to Madison, and three boys got their ears pierced, and they decided no more trips to Madison. So we went to town, and three of us saw this pizza place, Happy Pappy's." Attention seemed to be draining away, so I stepped up the pace. "So we ordered and paid, and they told us to come back in ten minutes. So we walked around the block or something, and when we came back, the lady handed us a *frozen* pizza. We were like, *What tha?* And she pointed to the sign, and under where it said Happy Pappy's, it said, 'We Make 'Em, You Bake 'Em'."

"So it wasn't a restaurant at all," Oliver said, obviously trying to help my story along. "It was a store that sold only frozen pizzas. That's the most fucked-up idea for a business that I've ever heard of since the Sansabelt. There's no way you could have known."

"Exactly. And they didn't even have an oven. We were going to ask the restaurant next door to cook our pizza for us, but we were too embarrassed. Then we were going to take it back to camp and, like, make a fire, but we didn't want to get back on the bus with this frozen pizza and have to explain what happened."

"So what'd you do?"

"We ate it!" Silence, clearly not the admiring kind. "Most of it, anyway. We were hungry. And pizza's pizza, and besides, it wasn't frozen solid or anything. It more like uncooked."

"I thought you said it was frozen."

Andrew slid down from the top bunk and pulled his Hammacher Schlemmer four-way flashlight from the shelf. "Here's what we're going to do," he announced. "This thing has an ultraviolet setting."

"So?"

"Semen glows under UV light."

All of us—campers and counselors included—reflexively covered our mattresses with our sleeping bags.

"Where did you hear that?" Max challenged. "First of all. And second of all, why do you have a flashlight that has ultraviolet?"

"It's got four settings—incandescent, halogen, xenon, and ultraviolet. It was a bar mitzvah present from my gentile Eagle Scout Uncle Chris." Andrew waved the flashlight in Max's direction. "And how do I know about UV and semen? My dad's firm handles sex crimes, okay?"

"So he's basically a professional pervert."

"That's what my mom says." We all watched as he lifted the lid on the pizza and wanded his hundred-and-eighty-dollar bar mitzvah present over the congealed mozzarella.

"It's too bright in here," he complained.

"Take it into Noah's Ark," I suggested. "No windows."

"Yeah, but then" Kyle said, "It's a pizza that's *been in* Noah's Ark. I'd rather just eat the jizzy pizza."

"Oliver," commanded Doron after the brief pause that followed that statement. "Try the pizza and tell us if it tastes like Mick's jizz."

Oliver's face clenched and he stood equidistant between Doron and the pizza, eyes locked on his nemesis. The smell of contempt almost overwhelmed the pizza smell.

"Go on, take it in your mouth, *bitch*."

The standoff contained the makings of a story that would be told for years to come. We all realized that we were present at the genesis of one of the great pizza stories in the history of Paley Lithwick Strauss, and the I-was-there value filled us with glory.

Oliver stood over the box, hands on hips. The wheels were turning. "I'll try the pizza, Doron," he said. "But I need a favor from you in return."

And that was how I found myself in downtown Chicago after midnight, double-parked in a pockmarked late-model Jaguar, with two minors as my passengers.

# PART VIII

Oliver, Tammy, and I had a lot to accomplish before we went in search of Rochelle. Oliver had to coach Doron in the task that only he could perform—obtaining the keys to the Jaguar. Tammy had to get twenty dollars from the office so we could afford gas and snacks. I had Hebrew to teach and services to lead. And we all had to make it through the rest of the afternoon and evening without telling anyone what we were planning.

During Hebrew, Rabbi Y'raeh sat us on the grass, withholding comments but clearly scrutinizing how I taught. We listened to a recording of and read the lyrics to "Hanasich Hakatan" by Yonatan Geffen, songwriter and nephew of Israel patriarch Moshe Dayan. Both Geffen's own experience as a paratrooper and Antoine de Saint-Exupéry's *The Little Prince* had inspired the song.

> *Veim ey pa'am tagiyu lechan*
> *Teydu she kan hu cheresh tzanach*
> *Vekol han'filah me'olam lo nishmah*
> *Biglal hachol harach.*

And if sometime you arrive here

Know that here he parachuted
And the sound of his fall was never heard
Because of the soft sand

The last time class met, we had read "The Giving Tree." So much had happened since then, it just made sense to tackle vocabulary and concepts on a higher level. Probably because of the senior rabbi's presence, but possibly because the material resonated with them, the campers showed actual life as they took turns with the verses. Even Max reined in the sarcasm. When we got through all the lyrics there were still ten minutes to kill, so I asked Rabbi Y'raeh, "Who is the most courageous person in the Torah?"

"Courage!" he spat. "What's that?"

"This song is about a brave paratrooper, right? So I was just thinking about Abraham and Moses and all those guys. They all had their own stuff to deal with, and, like, I thought maybe you had a favorite."

"Don't talk to me about courage," he said. "Talk about faith, compassion, justice, obeying the commandments. That's what counts to God. The rabbis call it *ometz lev*—courage of the *heart*."

"Yeah," I persisted, "But none of those things matter when you're jumping out of a plane."

"They most certainly do matter after you hit the ground, though. Were you a good person? Did you believe with all your heart? Did you care for your neighbor and show kindness to the weak? The rest… you can pay someone to do for you."

"Hire a goy, that's what my dad always says," Max concurred.

Tammy intervened. "Play the tape again, Eric. I want to hear the song again." The rabbi's face was impassive as Yonatan Geffen's voice came out the player. The grass tickled our legs while a breeze played with our hair and tantalized us with the smell of potatoes that the kitchen staff was deep-frying. "I think what Eric's asking," she said, gently touching his forearm, "is, What it was like for you in the camps?"

"My camp was just like your camp," he sniffed, tugging his sleeve down over the serial number.

"I seriously doubt that."

"I was," he began again, "Stupid then. Like all of you."

"Thanks a lot!"

"I mean, a teenager only. It's an incredible blessing to have made it from Treblinka to Wisconsin, to be sitting on the grass in a circle among you happy, healthy, stupid, wealthy young people."

"But really, what was it like? Nobody ever tells us anything."

"I had a job to do, putting one brick on top of the other. It wasn't easy, but mostly I cared about my friends. I cared about the pretty girls."

"What about your family?" Max asked.

"What family?" he cried, his eyes wild for a fleeting a moment. "We weren't heroes. We weren't brave. Some of us acted barbarically. There was no honor in it."

"We want to hear more about the girls," Tammy smiled.

"Now that you mention it," the rabbi responded. "There was a gypsy with big lips and rotten teeth."

"What was her name?"

In a susurrant tone he said, "Florica."

"I bet she could dance."

"Like a horse can run…. Would you play "Hanasich Hakatan" one more time, Eric? It's a beautiful song!"

We all felt lighter than air as the song played.

✡

Having soothed the savage rabbi, Tammy made quick work of obtaining the cash. She went to the office and explained to G'veret Greenbaum that I wanted to buy a floating heart necklace for Trina but had no money and was too embarrassed to speak up for myself. "He needs to show her he's really serious about her," she improvised. "She'll be at Brandeis, and he'll be at Northern Illinois, and a long-distance relationship needs a symbol like this to keep going. I'm really worried about him, actually. If he doesn't keep Trina, well, there aren't too many nice Jewish girls at Northern."

"Which one's Eric?" asked G'veret Greenbaum, a rotund woman with a soft spot for Jewish romance. (And a throbbing adoration for the Jewish state—it was she who had left the Beirut article on the library Xerox. She had been drafting a harsh retort.)

"Big nose?"

"Yeah…"

"Reddish hair?"

"No, that's Gregg with two g's. Eric's a skinny *machon* who plays guitar sometimes."

"Bad posture?"

"He looks like young tree," Tammy answered. "In a strong wind."

"The hunchback of Morton Grove," the administrator murmured, licking the pad of her thumb to peel off two of the crisp twenties clenched in her fist.

✡

Doron maintained that it would be easier just to snatch the car keys from Faber's purse, but Oliver insisted that she willingly hand them over. Touchingly, it was for my sake. Otherwise, as the one behind the wheel of

**85**

the Jaguar, I would be committing grand theft auto, a phrase he must have heard on TV.

"Then let *me* drive," Doron said.

The four of us conferred on the Lodge porch after evening services. Two counselors and two campers. Three males and a female. Three Americans and an Israeli. We each had different interests at stake and different amounts of leverage with the others. Doron's smashed-in face resembled a jack-o-lantern in the dying Wisconsin twilight. Aided by eyeliner, Oliver could have passed for a matinee idol, were it not for that enormous forehead.

"You're an awful driver," I told Doron. "Because you learned to drive on the other side of the road."

"No I didn't. We read right to left, that's what you're thinking of."

"Anyway, we need someone to watch our cabin."

"What's going to happen? Someone's going to kidnap a camper?"

"Isn't that the whole reason we're here?"

"So what do I say?"

A cloud of gnats engulfed us as we spitballed ruses. Tammy needed an abortion. Tammy had to return an engagement ring to an ex-boyfriend who needed to pawn it so he could pay off his bookie. Tammy's mother was dying of ovarian cancer and wanted to see her one last time. Oliver paced up and down the porch. "Say you're on a mission from God."

We all wrinkled our brows.

"I'm serious! This is top-secret Israeli Army shit. She'll go nuts for that. You need to deliver a sealed envelope to your contact in the lobby of the Drake Hotel at exactly midnight. The envelope contains the blueprints for…"

"What's the PLO equivalent of the Death Star?" I asked.

"Exactly!

"Exactly what?"

"This is the whole reason you're even a counselor, Doron. Why else would you be here? You're going to waste a whole summer teaching American kids to shoot penalty kicks? Fuck that, you're here to serve your country."

"So romantic," gushed Tammy. "Undercover shit!"

"Massively undercover," continued Oliver. "Thanks to U.S. satellite technology, a secret weapons cache has been pinpointed in southern Lebanon, and you need to deliver the coordinates to an agent based in Chicago."

"I'll do it," agreed Doron. "But Eric, you need to barge in exactly three minutes after I go in there. She can't have too much time to think, or she'll realize how stupid it is."

"I'll make up the envelope," Oliver offered. "If she hesitates, start to show her, but then don't. She'll just see rubber stamp marks all over it. Tell her you don't want to put her in any danger."

Doron held his head in his hands. "We can only hope Faber will cream in her pants for this stuff as much as Tammy is."

"Who said anything about creaming? What am I, a dairy cow? I swear, guys are so ignorant about female anatomy."

✡

I waited the requisite three minutes but knocked on the wrong door.

The room wouldn't come into focus, and though it was immediately apparent that Doron and Faber weren't in here, that wasn't the reason I regretted getting the room number wrong. There was a queen-sized bed against the wall, sheets tangled. The blinds were drawn, but the setting sun angled narrow beams through the gaps, painting a cloud of tobacco smoke with bright stripes and tracing the contours of the figure sitting up on the mattress.

"Hi?" I said, shielding my eyes and turning to face the doorframe.

"Hello," she replied.

"I didn't know you smoked," I said.

"Only when I'm nervous," my mother said, pulling the blankets tighter around her shoulders. One corner of the fitted sheet was coming off the mattress.

Rabbi Mick's voice came from a smoke-shrouded corner of the room. "Eric, it's time for evening prayers. The campers are waiting for you."

# PART IX

The other boys cabin led the "Home"-themed service. I ruefully strummed the chords to "Homeward Bound" as they mumbled their original meditations.

*Being here at camp, away from my home, makes me appreciate my home more than ever. Home is more than an address. It's who you are.*

*Some people say it's your DNA that makes you who you are. Others say it's the environment you grow up in—in other words, your home. I think it's about half and half. Please rise for the Barchu*

*Last year my class took a field trip to a homeless shelter. It really made me think about how lucky I am to have a roof over my head. Please rise for the Sh'ma.*

✡

Whatever had transpired between Doron and Faber had undermined his *sabra* cockiness. His torso seemed to have shrunken, or his Israel is Real t-shirt had enlarged. Shakily he pushed the car keys across the dining hall table and then contemplated the palm of his hand before starting a sentence two or three times and then reconsidering.

"You okay, Doron?"

"What? Yeah, great."

"Well, thanks." I said. "Wish us luck tonight."

"You got a driver's license?

"Yep."

"Money?"

"Uh-huh." The Jaguar keys were chained to a miniature sterling spoon.

"What about a map? Do you even know where you're going?"

"It shouldn't be that hard to find Chicago," I replied. "The tricky part will be finding Rochelle."

The sound of her name snapped Doron out of his torpor. "Fuck Rochelle. Just go out and have fun," he advised. "Don't waste your night on that rich bitch. In fact…." He dug his wallet out his jeans.

"I told you, we've got money."

Out of his wallet came something small and almost flat, a foil packet about the size of a Saltine. He laid it down beside the keys. "You know how to use one of these?"

"Pretty much," I said.

"Need me to demonstrate?"

"No thanks," I huffed. "I got it."

✡

Putting the cabin to sleep with a recording of "War of the Worlds" was my bad idea. The idea was to hit "play" and then quietly pack for the journey while they drifted off to dreamland, but Orson Welles's radio play proved more frightful than anticipated. By the time the fake announcer declared:

> *Good heavens, something's wriggling out of the shadow like a gray snake. Now it's another one, and another. They look like tentacles to me. There, I can see the thing's body. It's large, large as a bear and it glistens like wet leather.*

it was past time to turn it off and counteract the effect with some soothing George Winston piano. Andrew had puked into a Rubbermaid garbage bucket, Max had insisted he'd seen a "lady with a club" approaching from the direction of the Lodge, invoking a mythical bloody figure dating back to the origins of Paley Lithwick. Other boys suddenly recalled a series of sharp metallic clanks the night before.

After repeatedly reassuring the boys that they *hadn't* seen or heard anything and that there was *nothing* out there, I absented myself. The plan was to pull the car up to the gate and wait for Oliver and Tammy, but on my way out the door I bumped into Jason Harris.

"Where do you think you're going?" he asked.

"I think I'm coming down with something. I'm going to snag some Nyquil from the Lodge and hit the sack."

"Not tonight you don't."

"Huh?"

"Don't tell me your forgot your own bar mitzvah!"

There was no talking my way out of this sacred obligation. Drinking shots in front of my friends took precedence over saving a human life. Oliver conceded the point and offered to send word to Tammy that the Mission from God would be postponed twenty-four hours.

En route to the Stockyard, I found myself worrying that Rochelle would turn up and I wouldn't get to search for her after all. Does the desire to do something invalidate its courage? It would seem so. All I wanted was an adventure.

✡

"Friends, Hebrews, Countrymen," Jason began, one hand on my shoulder, the other raising the triangle rack high above his head. "Why is tonight is different from all other nights? Why do we assemble in this godforsaken establishment, suffering skunked beer, medieval restrooms, and the hostile glances of townies? Why do we tend to the children of privilege, struggling to overcome their indifference? Why do we bother trying to inculcate them with respect for our heritage when every cell in their bodies is saturated with sex hormones?"

Hoots of affirmation came from the circle of onlookers. Trina was up front cheering, her dark eyes shining with affection or something more carnal, though we hadn't been alone together since the bagel incident.

"This young man before you," Jason continued, slipping the triangular rack over my head, "is the living embodiment of the definitive answer to this age-old question. Last summer, he was one of *them*. Tonight, he is one of *us*. Last summer, he slept in a sleeping bag on a bunk bed. This summer, he sleeps in sheets on a cot. The boy who used to follow is now a man who leads." Applause battered my eardrums like a hard rain on a cabin roof as four counselors heaved me onto the foosball table. Someone handed me a champagne flute. My Jewish nose impeded sipping, so I had to throw my head back.

"Speech!" demanded Trina.

"Drop trou'!" demanded Doron.

I contemplated belting out "Tradition," but looking down the length of the bar, I noticed Detective Hanekamp hunched over a Rolling Rock. Inciting a re-enactment of *Fiddler on the Roof* in front of this Aryan authority figure felt all wrong. For an instant, my balance faltered, and I nearly pitched forward into the arms of my fellow counselors.

Trina approached, her face lit up with maternal concern, but I waved her off and grasped the pool cue like a microphone. "Thank you, Jason," I said. "Thank you, all. It's a great honor to be called to the holy foosball table." It wasn't too late to go searching for Rochelle. One single dose of champagne had hit my brain, but I could still manage the wheel of the Jaguar if I got out now. Maybe I would take the pool cue with me, as a weapon. If you swung them from the thin end, the thick end could easily crack a skull.

The words were forming but not coming out of my mouth. *Thank you, friends, sort-of friends, and girls I wish I could fondle, but this is no time for drunken antics or religious mockery. The Talmud says whoever saves a life, it is considered as if he saved an entire world, so if you'll excuse me....*

"Bellybutton shot!" hollered Doron, as if he knew what I was about to do and had been hit by the stroke of genius required to make me stay. "Trina! ... No, Cheryl! Cheryl, get up on the bar and lie flat on your back. Trust me, this is a Talmudic emergency."

Cheryl bounced into position without a moment's hesitation. In cut-off jeans and a ribbed Gap tank top, she seemed to relish the role of the virgin (or close enough) sacrifice displayed on the bar-slash-altar. She giggled as Doron sprinkled table salt on her left thigh and complied as he wedged a lime wedge into her cleavage. Trina looked crestfallen.

"Bar mitzvah boy," he called. "Prepare yourself for the sacred ritual of the bellybutton shot. Not a single droplet can remain, or you have to do it all over again." He ordered a shot of Cuervo and muttered a quick blessing as Cheryl awaited the anointment, body writhing, abdominals rippling. At the end of the bar, Hanekamp raised his mug in my direction.

✡

Despite a brain soaked through with alcohol and lust, I managed a moment alone with him before leaving the Stockyard and told him we were going in search of Rochelle the first chance we got the next day. He claimed to have lost all interest in the case.

"What about finding people within forty-eight hours of their disappearance?" I said. "What about the Book of Life?"

"Not my book, not my life," he said, sliding a white rectangle along the bar toward me. The card was ivory, a heavy stock, unembellished. The cursive, small and vaguely European.

> R: *Your father doesn't need to know about this. I am sending you these things to put on to make absolutely sure we won't be recognized. I am getting a dye job and a new used car. Get ready for a mother-daughter (and Crockett) adventure.*

"Where did you get this?"

"Remember the shoebox?"

"That's it, then," I conceded. "Case closed."

"The word is but a clue," Hanekamp intoned. "The real burden of understanding is upon the mind and soul of the reader."

"What's that?"

"Abraham Joshua Heschel, *God in Search of Man.* I can read, too, Eric. Does that bother you?"

"I guess I was looking forward to the adventure. Stupid, I know."

"Nobody knows about this card but you, me, and Marguerite La Vraie Strauss. Go 'find' her if you want."

"Where do I look?"

"Check the second story."

"Second story of what?"

"Strauss comma Franklin."

# NUMBERS

# PART I

Stories like this often conclude with where-are-they-now updates, and though this one is still going, now seems like the right time to get that part over with.

Oliver Berkowitz became a big deal in real estate. He pretty much colonized Oakland for the techies and made a second fortune in karaoke bars. He lives in a converted printing plant with his partner, an Italian landscape architect. For a few months they had a mutt named Rabbi Mick, but it ran away.

Tammy is a massage therapist, pretty much orthodox now, with a dash of paganism. She's got seven kids—three biological, three adopted from Malawi, one a mystery—all of their Hebrew names are tattooed on her back. She knits yarmulkes, belongs to a feminist book club, and avoids gluten, refined sugar, and negative people. I know the most about her life because she posts every little thing on Facebook. We run into each other every now and then, and I have to act like whatever she tells me is a big surprise.

I am a certified financial planner, which, as I constantly have to explain, is different from a certified public accountant. My job is helping people make sound decisions with their money, which means steering clear of investing in startups, hedge funds, derivatives, and junk bonds—all the goodies I gorged upon after inheriting a tidy sum in my twenties. Pretty much nobody with real wealth listens to me. My wife and kids think I'm a god, though.

Doron Ba'al Shem Tov became an activist in Israel. It doesn't matter which side he was on, except to the thugs who set his home on fire a few years into the new century, incinerating everyone inside. After the summer of 1986, I never saw him again, but I attended a ceremony dedicating the memorial garden in Jerusalem that Oliver commissioned.

Doron's is the sole death in this story. Rochelle turned out fine; her intermediate whereabouts and condition will be detailed shortly. In the long run, she studied business at Emory and remained in Atlanta to operate an executive recruitment firm. She serves as president of her congregation and devotes her vacations to parasailing and Jet Skis. For many years I sent cards and then emails on our birthday, but they were rarely reciprocated or acknowledged. The last time we saw each other, while we danced at a celebration of her parents' fiftieth wedding anniversary, she insisted that if she had indeed saved my life on the lake, she would definitely have remembered it.

✡

*The second story.* I tried to analyze Hanekamp's clue—avoiding any mention of the note he'd shown me—with Tammy and Oliver as we sped due south on Interstate 94 East under crystalline skies. They both sat in the back, pawing through the shoebox Faber had left behind. The moonroof was open, so we had to raise our voices.

"What's the difference between a sunroof and a moonroof?" I asked, but neither replied. Tammy was shaving her legs—dry—while Oliver flipped through the nightlife listings in the back of the *Chicago* magazine that had been left in the backseat.

"I'm thirsty," Tammy said when she was finished.

"Can I put a tape in?" Oliver asked, leaning forward to insert The Cramps' *Bad Music for Bad People*. Naturally, he had brought his valise of cassettes.

> *I've learned all I know*
> *By the age of nine*
> *But I could better myself*
> *If I could only find*

"We can find the Strauss' home address," I said. "But she won't be there. Maybe there's a Strauss Management or a Strauss Incorporated in the Yellow Pages. Maybe there's a business on the first floor and something else on the 'second story'."

"What kind of something else?" Oliver challenged.

"Hell if I know," I sighed. "Hanekamp said it was on the second story."

> *Some new kind of kick*
> *Some—* [Israeli flatulence]
> *Some new kind of buzz*
> *I wanna go hog mad*

"Let's stop, I'm thirsty," Tammy said.

"Great America!" Oliver screamed. "Two more exits."

"Hell, no," I said.

"C'mon! There's a stand that sells Faygo Floats. It's the most sugar you can legally fit into a 16-ounce cup."

"We're driving to Chicago to rescue Rochelle, remember?"

"But first, a Faygo Float."

"Perfect," I said, "That's just a little too perfect."

"What's that supposed to mean?"

"Nothing, I just said we're not stopping at a theme park on the way to rescuing Rochelle."

I glanced at the speedometer and realized we were doing 90. This vehicle had a few more horses under the hood than I was used to. The other cars on the highway seemed to be standing still. The air rushing through the moonroof drowned out the stereo.

"Put it down, Oliver," Tammy cautioned. "He's pulling over at Great America."

A bright orange shape loomed in the rearview mirror. Pointing Faber's flare pistol at my head with one hand, Oliver used the other to cock it.

Easing off the gas, I observed the farmlands unblurring, felt the rushing in my ears subside, making space for the Cramps' psychobilly throb. For some reason the deceleration made me conscious of the condom, Doron's gift to me, crinkling in the front pocket of my shorts. The orange shape dropped out of view, and it came to me that I was never going back to Paley Lithwick Strauss. Not the next day. Not ever.

That's what home is. The place—and time—you can't return to.

Z-Force, Great America's newest ride, had replaced the previous newest ride, the Edge, which had malfunctioned and sent a few thrill seekers to the hospital the summer before. Sucking on our Faygo Floats, we stood in the line behind two shaggy dudes dressed completely in mismatched denim, one tall with clear skin, one heavy with mint green eyes and a gold stud in his left earlobe. They looked a little older than me, but they didn't strike me as college students. They were debating *Top Gun*.

"Yeah but even Maverick couldn't, like, *stop* in mid-air."

"Of course, you can, dude. You just hit the air brakes."

"Dude, there's no such thing as air brakes," the heavy one asserted, before turning to Tammy and asking if he knew her from somewhere.

"I'm pretty famous," she said. "Got my own sitcom, my own line of cosmetics."

"She's shitting you," the tall one notified his friend. "She's lucky she's hot."

"Or what?" Oliver sneered. "If she wasn't hot you'd slap her upside the head?"

"Not me. I'm Mahatma fucking Gandhi."

"That's perfect because I'm Albert fucking Schweitzer," Oliver answered. "It's like the whole Nobel fucking Peace prize roster is in line for Z-Force today."

"You are hot, though," continued the heavy one. "But I bet you're cool, too. Do you and your brothers partake?"

"We're not her—" I started.

"What a coincidence," Oliver cracked a few beats late. "We have the same middle name."

"—We might," Tammy said.

From inside his jacket, the heavy one fished a wax-paper sandwich bag half-filled with misshapen brown nuggets.

"*Fucking*," Oliver clarified.

"What are those supposed to be?" I asked.

"Space Balls," he whispered. "You can't light up in the park, but you can eat one of these. I used my great-grandma's homemade malted milk ball recipe. They got a little smooshed inside my jacket, sorry."

Before I knew it, Tammy and Oliver had both gobbled a Space Ball. Before I gave it too much thought, so had I.

"That tasted," Oliver declared, "exactly like a rabbit pellet, if a gigantic, irradiated rabbit had been fed a steady diet of the grass that grows on Milton S. Hershey's grave."

"By any chance are you guys Jewish?"

"By any chance are you guys Nazis?"

"No."

"Then yes, we are. Was it the horns that gave us away?"

"You have horns?"

"That's a myth," I explained. "And before you ask, we don't use the blood of gentile children to make matzos."

"Not anymore, anyway," added Oliver. "The new recipe calls for menstrual blood from gentile adolescents."

"Your brothers are wasted already," the tall one said, turning away. The Denim Brothers were the last two to be admitted onto the next Z-Force, which meant we were at the head of the line for the one after that, so two of us could sit in the front car. Oliver argued that since he and Tammy had been sitting in the back of the Jag, they deserved the two seats up front, and I did not object.

My seatmate was a middle-aged woman in mirrored shades and a B. Kliban cat-themed sweat suit, who had seemingly come to Great America by herself. "Puke on me," she warned, "And I throw you off this thing." A quick and mirthless laugh attested to her seriousness as the mechanical restraints engaged. During the slow initial climb, Oliver and Tammy spontaneously began chanting "*Dah-veed Melech Yisrael.*" It became clear to me—I couldn't tell how long the realization had been waiting for me to acknowledge it—that my two campers knew something I didn't. Probably it was a secret about Rochelle. Luring me here was part of their overall plan.

We crested, shuddered, and shot downward, corkscrewing one way and then the other. My companion made orgasmic sounds with each hairpin, while Tammy and Oliver continued to yelp Hebrew lyrics, but the motions of the ride did not affect me. I occupied an impossibly dense Copernican center as rollercoaster and park orbited all around. The velocity of each twist dreamed up by the ride's designers disappointed me with its sheer obviousness. It almost felt like I was controlling Z-Force rather than the other way around—up until the very end, which felt like being sucker-punched by a brick wall.

"Guess crying is better than puking," the cat lady sneered as she heaved herself out of the car. The back of my hand coated with snot and tears, I stumbled away from the ride and raced back to a payphone that I recalled had been beside the Faygo stand.

"I would like to reverse the charges," I told the operator, giving her my dad's number in Dallas. After three rings the machine picked up.

"This call can't go through," the operator apologized.

"Please!" I said, conscious of the moisture in my voice. "I need to tell my dad something."

"Just this once," the operator said, just before an automated voice said to wait for the tone.

"Dad," I sobbed. "It's Eric. Everything's okay, but I want you to know, I'm going into Chicago today. In case anyone needs to know where I am. The camp is sending me. I'm not sure of the number where I'll be staying tonight, somewhere downtown probably, but maybe I'll call you when I find out, so if you want to reach me you'll know how to." I caught my breath and went on. "Anyway, I hope you don't mind that I called collect. It's just that something happened at camp, and a girl ran away or was taken away, and the camp wants me to help, because they said I know her better than anybody else, so I would have the best chance of finding her. It's not like I left the campers alone or anything. I'm not even a full counselor, actually. I'm a *machon*, a junior counselor. The main counselor is this Israeli guy, Doron, who's on duty in case there's something to the 'Lady with the Club' legend after all."

And then the most egregious non sequitur to ever emerge from my lips: "Mom says hi."

"I'm sure they're fine," I forged ahead after a pause. "It's really the girl we're worried about. Or at least I am. You've probably heard of her dad, Franklin Strauss. They just changed the name of the camp to Paley Lithwick *Strauss* because he donated a lot of money, so it would look kind of bad if they lost his daughter."

The phone was silent. Tammy and Oliver stood a few feet away, quizzical looks on their faces. I couldn't tell if my message had been cut off, either by the machine or by the operator.

"Rochelle is her name," I said before replacing the receiver.

# PART II

Heading into the legendary skyline as the summer sun set, I still hadn't succeeded in getting Tammy and Oliver to focus on what we would actually do when we got to Chicago. Oliver was holding forth on his personal John Hughes theory.

"He's not what people think he is at all. Sure, there are teenagers in his movies, but they are just props."

"Is that why the actors are all in their thirties?"

"He's a deeply religious filmmaker—a holy man. You can tell from his choice of music. Every song expresses something even more rarefied than man's search for God. It's God's yearning for man. Without us he's nothing. Take 'If You Leave,' from *Pretty in Pink*.

"*Orchestral Manoeuvres* in the Dark," I said.

"Exactly! As a love song, it's incoherent, but as a plea from a dejected deity, it's marvelous." He popped the tape in.

*If you leave, don't leave now*
*Please don't take my heart away*
*Promise me, just one more night*
*Then we'll go our separate ways*
*We've always had time on our side*
*Now it's fading fast*
*Every second, every moment*
*We've gotta make it last*

"And then of course there's *The Breakfast Club* theme."

*Will you stand above me?*
*Look my way, never love me*
*Rain keeps falling, rain keeps falling*
*Down, down, down*
*Will you recognize me?*
*Call my name or walk on by*
*Rain keeps falling, rain keeps falling*
*Down, down, down, down*

"I love that song," Tammy said. "But I thought it was about the popular kids not saying hi to you in the hall."

"A common misconception," he replied, before adding with a flourish, "You might have missed this hymn from *Sixteen Candles*."

> *If you were here*
> *I could deceive you*
> *And if you were here*
> *You would believe*

"I'm hungry," Tammy said. "And someone in this car needs a shower."

"It's Oliver," I said. "He's trying to make sure God can smell him."

The Kennedy Expressway grew increasingly congested as we approached Downtown, but speed didn't matter much since we didn't know where to go. Between us we had $12—enough for a meal but not a hotel room. I considered driving to my house in Morton Grove but didn't want to face my mom, if she was back, and besides, the idea of Home contradicted the spirit of the Trip. It was a mission without purpose, an investigation in search of a procedure. The unexamined romance of it all was making me fall in love, a little bit, with Tammy Hamelin. It wasn't just the way she filled out a cut-off ZBT sweatshirt. It was the future she unveiled for me, a life we could share together, a family we could raise.

*Where did you two meet? Actually, he was my summer camp cou—*

This reverie nudged my attention off the road, and I didn't recover in time when the Brink's truck in front of us hit the brakes. "How am I driving?" the bumper sticker inquired, ironically, just as the shoulder harness dug into my flesh. The sensation of impact powerfully recalled the Z-Force's abrupt conclusion. Why one should be thrilling and the other tragic was beyond explanation.

"Everyone okay?" I asked as I pulled over behind the truck.

"What are we going to say?" Oliver asked.

"To who?" Tammy said. "The guy we hit?"

"To the cops. When they pull up and ask Mario Andretti up there what he's doing with two minors in the back seat, especially once they force us to pee in a cup."

"Just hold it in," I said, as if I'd been subjected to a police-ordered drug test before.

We quickly cobbled together a story. This was Victoria Faber's Jaguar. (There was no way around that. Her name was on the registration.) She had lent it to me so I could take Tammy to see her mother, who was dying of ovarian cancer. Oliver had come along because he was her best friend. The driver of the truck, a wiry black man in coveralls, hopped out with an unexpected grin plastered on his face.

"Shit, boy, don't you know better than to interrupt the All-Star Game? The Rocket is pitching a perfect game."

"I am so sorry. Can I, um, give you my phone number and we can work this out later?"

"I've got plenty of numbers already, sport."

His truck, which was built to withstand far more impact than I had inflicted, looked good as new. The fender of the Jaguar, on the other hand, dangled dangerously close to the pavement.

"Baseball sucks!" Oliver shouted.

Tammy and me in love. Backpacking around Europe, climbing ruins, tasting strange liqueurs. A seaside wedding under the stars. Painting the nursery together. Our children gathered around for the lighting of the Sabbath candles.

Or maybe there was something in the Space Balls.

The fact that those two Neanderthals at Great America assumed I was Tammy's brother should have confirmed that she was out of reach. My driver's license was the only reason I got to hang out with her at all, and I had just proved myself unworthy of it. There was a better chance of my killing her in a crash than marrying her on the beach.

We finally parked in a garage near Union Station and used the duct tape, which Faber had thoughtfully left behind, to secure the fender. It looked like botched surgery, and most of the right headlamp was now masked, but it would suffice. We took over a booth in Lou Mitchell's, a Naugahyde deli famous for large helpings and Milk Duds handed out by chewing gum-snapping, wisecrack-making waitresses.

Ours, in truth, was on the surly side. As she wiped the z-shaped counter with a gray rag, she said the soup of the day was beef minestrone, but she clearly didn't think we'd order it in a thousand years. There was a kind of room divider lined with potted plants, and on the other side was what looked like a giant multi-chamber aquarium. Tammy asked what it was.

"Water filter. Can I take your order?"

"Could I have a side order of fries, please, Maxine," I said, reading the pin on her uniform. "Even if I'm not ordering a main course?"

"Just this once," she said. "Anything to drink with that?"

"A glass of water, please." When she scowled, I hurriedly added, "It just looks so refreshing," sending Tammy and Oliver into hysterics, which Maxine clearly resented. She didn't cheer up any when they declined to order anything.

Tammy found a phone book in the foyer and was leafing through the Str-'s as we picked at our fries. "*Straight from Heaven Nails, Strange Brew Beverage Co., Street-Life Footwear.* No Strauss."

"What does he do, anyway?"

"He owns a printing press," answered Oliver. "He uses it to print money around the clock."

"Franklin Strauss is in private equity," Tammy said.

"Like you even know what that means," Oliver said.

"Rochelle said it's like," Tammy began, "when all the guys sit in a circle on the floor and…" (making a gesture with her wrist) "on a cracker."

"You can get paid for that?" Oliver said in disbelief.

"It's a metaphor," I offered.

"Right," she said. "At first, one guy's doing it as hard as he can, and then this other guy's racing to catch up, and then another guy tries to get in on the action. One of them has to finish last, and he gets stuck eating the cookie."

"I thought you said cracker."

"Whatever. Private equity is avoiding being that guy."

The metaphor tried to ruin my appetite, but the munchies overpowered it. Rather than satisfying my hunger, the fries just made me want more fries. A long-hidden irritability burst forth, convinced that answers could be had if questions were asked forcefully enough. "What happened in Milwaukee?" I asked. "What happened with Rochelle and her dad?"

Tammy started playing with a grease stain on her placemat. "She found something out about him."

"I'm listening."

"How she found out wasn't how he wanted her to find out," Oliver added without clarifying.

"Is he some kind of criminal?"

"Why would you say that?"

"Behind every great fortune is a great crime. I read it somewhere."

"It's more a sin than a crime," Tammy said.

The waitress came by with Milk Duds, probably trying to get us to pay and leave, but the memory of the Space Balls was too fresh for us to accept and we pocketed them for later.

"Actually," Oliver said, "Until 1962 it was *both,* in the State of Illinois."

"What was both? C'mon, you guys."

"Well," Tammy said, plucking the last fry off the plate, "You know that guy who was with Mr. Strauss? The waterski guy?"

"Let me guess," I guessed, a little too quickly. "They were fucking."

Naïveté is especially comical when it pretends to be its opposite. I could tell from their embarrassed laughter that what I'd missed was glaringly obvious. "Well," Oliver finally replied, "*Someone* was."

Tammy patted my wrist. "Rochelle really liked Serge and thought he liked her back. After he told her about the boat show in Milwaukee, she called her dad and asked him to take her. At first, when they got there and met up with him, everything was hunky-dory."

Oliver leapt to his feet. "Pause right there. I just remembered something, but I don't want to miss this. Eric, can I see the car key?"

"You want me to give you the key to the Jaguar."

"Yeah, I just have to get something. What, do you think I'm going to drive away or something?"

"You need to get something."

"Right."

"And then you'll be back."

"I promise," he said.

"He promises," Tammy said. "I promise too."

I handed over the key and put my head down on the table, groaning, "Where are we going to sleep tonight? We don't have enough money for a hotel. We should have gotten more cash from G'veret Greenbaum."

"I've slept three to a car before. The two front seats both recline far enough, and the tallest one gets the back."

"How many nights can we sleep in a Jaguar in a parking garage?" I asked. Realizing the futility of this whole enterprise, I almost lost interest in what had happened to Rochelle in Milwaukee.

Oliver was out of breath when he returned, and grinning like a fool. He flashed a Diner's Club card. "Look what was in the glove compartment. How did we not look there?"

"Oliver!"

"What. Is this not a diner?" He beckoned Maxine and ordered the beef stroganoff from the seldom-traveled Entrées section of the menu. Following suit, Tammy got the shrimp de jonghe, and I got the chicken cordon bleu. What can I say—it was a night to take risks. Maxine called us sweethearts.

"So anyway, Milwaukee," Oliver said.

"Rochelle, Frank, and Serge were looking at the boats," Tammy continued. "And asking questions about prices and features and all that. Serge suggested dinner, and they agreed to meet at seven. Rochelle's dad gave her a $100 bill to shop for a dress."

"She's a fast shopper," Oliver added. "She can go through a hundred bucks in no time flat."

"Right," Tammy said. "So she got back to the hotel fast. Faster than her dad expected."

"And he must have forgotten she had the room key. He had other things on his mind," Oliver said. And then they both looked at me, waiting for a picture to sink in.

My throat tightened, fighting my next question. "So Rochelle's dad… and the Brazilian guy were…"

"All she actually saw," Oliver grinned, "was a tan, waxed, muscular blur leaping from the bed to the closet."

"Who's going to sign for the credit card?" I asked. We took turns scribbling *Franklin J. Strauss* on our placemats until we decided my forgery came the closest to the signature on the back of the card.

"How did you know the credit card would be in the glove compartment?" I asked.

"Actually, that's not what I went back for," he said, producing the *Chicago* magazine that he had been reading in the back seat.

We turned to him.

"What Hanekamp said. Look."

> **Second Story.** *157 E Ohio St #2.* Open till 2 a.m. In this dimly lit, discreet Streeterville saloon, elegantly attired stockbrokers sip cognac alongside beer-swilling bricklayers and daring grad students.

# PART III

In the weeks before college, when I should have been packing and preparing, bidding farewells and refreshing my wardrobe, I spent way too many hours in my bedroom, shades drawn, writing and rewriting a song about that night. The idea was less to narrate the event than to capture the essence of a moment that contained volumes of contradictory information. It was my "American Pie" (or better yet, "American chai"), complete with coded lyrics and shifting time signatures.

> *You were out hunting the mermaid.*
> *The mermaid was hunting the fox.*
> *The fox sailed away, down South, so they say,*
> *And nobody answers your knocks.*

A check came from the camp, $250, paying me for my work. Disappointingly, it was signed by G'veret Greenbaum, not Mick Harris. I spent most of my earnings at 7-Eleven on Pringles and Skoal Bandits, these little pouches of moistened tobacco that fit between your teeth and lower lip. The nicotine kept me just the right amount of angry, and after a while I managed to stop myself from chewing through the pouch. The Chicago Cubs coffee mug on my desk filled with brown juice as verse after verse tapped out on my Selectric.

The first time I committed "The Very Narrow Bridge" to tape, it went on for nearly twelve minutes. One verse depicts "a hurricane of herring, tearing through the Dairyland." Another envisions the song itself playing on the mermaid's car radio, her pulling over and resting her head on the steering wheel, "trying to decide just what not to feel." Between the third verse and the chorus comes a down-tempo passage in a minor key:

*If you want to know if we ever caught the crook,*
*You can look up the answer in my unwritten book.*

✡

Tammy, Oliver, and I got back in the car and drove to the intersection of Ohio and St. Clair. An Armenian restaurant occupied the supposed address of the bar, which perplexed us until we realized that Second Story was, of course, on the second story. "Wasn't there an Armenian genocide or something?" I said as I parallel parked between a pickup truck and an empty taxi.

"Does that mean the Armenians were genoci*ding* or genoci*ded*?" Oliver pondered.

"Remind me again why we think Rochelle's here," Tammy said.

"All I know," I answered, "Is I'm not going up there." I threw the car into reverse.

"None of us is," Oliver said as I tapped—well, more than tapped—the taxi. "And are you trying to genocide Strauss's car or something?"

"So we're just going to wait until someone comes out?" I wondered whether a Diner's Club card would work in a gas station.

"Not exactly," he said. "We're sending Claire Standish." In a flash he had pulled on the mauve scrubs and the red wig and sprung out of the Jaguar, applying lipstick while strutting to the door.

"I can't believe this," I said.

"Me either," Tammy said. "He forgot to change his shoes. Claire Standish most certainly does not wear Chuck Taylors."

I killed the engine but left the key in the ignition and put *Songs from the Big Chair* in the tape player. Humidity made the stoplights twinkle like UFOs. It was nearly eleven o'clock, and the streets were nearly empty. Three guys in almost-matching outfits—white oxford, paisley necktie, suspenders, pleated slacks, tasseled shoes—started to approach us but veered away. Halfway into "Everybody Wants to Rule the World," Tammy leaned forward between the seats and hit eject. "Why do guys constantly have to have music playing?" she demanded.

"Because real life needs a cool soundtrack."

"Come back here and put your arm around me," she said. "It's getting cold."

"I could close this." We looked up and the mist-haloed full moon seemed to be balanced on the highest plateau of the Sears Tower.

"Just get back here already."

We kissed for a long time, maybe five minutes. Her skills exceeded mine, but I basically kept up. If driving away with two campers hadn't already sealed my fate, this backseat makeout master class would have guaranteed permanent banishment from Paley Lithwick. Saliva didn't erase the bright line between staff and camper. On the contrary, physical affection inherently constituted assault.

A hot wind blew through my mind, accompanied by images of Rabbi Mick flashlight-tapping on the window as my hair wound around Tammy's fingers. Her eyes stayed closed—I knew because mine were open. The three tasseled guys remained, just about ten or twelve feet away, conferring among themselves. They all stood about the same height, but from their postures I could identify one as the ringleader, one as the instigator, and one as the coward.

Through the windshield I noticed a window to the Second Story, but nothing was visible in it but blue lights alternating with rhythmic pink flashes. "What are they doing up there?" I said, pulling away.

"The Electric Slide," she answered. "The Cabbage Patch."

"Should I go up?" I asked.

"Oliver can handle himself."

"Here's the thing," I said, completely ignorant of what the thing was. "So can Rochelle. There's absolutely no reason to think she's hanging out in Downtown Chicago at a gay bar." (The last two words came out as a whisper.) "Wherever she is, she probably wants to be there. Whatever she's doing, she probably wants to be doing it. We just threw our lives away—at least I did—because of her, and meanwhile we couldn't be farther from her mind. In fact, I should have shown you this already."

"Eric, don't!"

"It's not *that*," I pouted. "It's a note from her mom."

I took out the card, but to my surprise, Tammy recognized it. "Did Hanekamp give that to you?"

"How did you know?"

"I gave it to him."

"So we're just out here for..."

"The *romance*," she smiled.

"Good," I sighed. "If she were missing, and we found her, what were we even going to do about it? Shoot the bad guys with a flare gun?" I felt around in the dark for the gun. "Wait, where is that thing?"

"It probably just fell under the seat," Tammy said. "We don't have to be heroes. We're just trying to help our friend, even if she doesn't know or care. Besides, I really like you," Tammy smiled, taking my hands in hers. "You look great when you're playing guitar, and you have a certain sort of honesty that most guys aren't capable of, and a kindness that most guys would be afraid to show."

"You've kissed like half the guys in my cabin, haven't you?" I said, badly miscalculating the type of honesty she appreciated, and she folded her arms across her chest.

"Sorry, Tammy," I tried. "That didn't come out how I meant it."

"It was my fault for thinking you could be kind *and* honest."

"It came out all wrong."

"You're right about one thing though," she said. "The flare gun isn't back here."

"Wow," I gulped. "What does Oliver think he's doing?" I started to shift in my seat to get a better view when Tammy's hand darted between my legs.

"My bad!" she grinned as I leapt up. "I could have sworn this was the flare gun."

"Gentle, Tammy!" With self-conscious laughter, I added, "It could go off when you least expect it." It worried me so much that her wandering fingers might discover the condom in my shorts that I barely knew how to register her advance.

"You think I'm a slut."

"I didn't say that."

"You didn't have to."

"I wouldn't."

"You sort of did."

"There are worse things to be," I said. We started kissing again, but in a minor key now. The instigator of the tassel trio was humping the coward's side while the ringleader doubled over with laughter.

"I do tend to get carried away," she admitted. "It's been like that ever since my mom got sick. Her cancer has made me hyper aware of my own equipment, in all its majesty. It's like a tingling alarm that goes off every hour. Sometimes at night I wonder if I'll ever get to sleep."

"Me too. Every guy I know."

"Yeah, but guys are supposed to think with their dicks. A chick who thinks with her clit is a slut."

"I never said that!"

"At least you're a gentleman," she went on. "You're not doing this just to have something to brag about. I was with somebody recently. I don't want to say his name, because you know him. At one point I licked my palm, and..." (A warning look from her stopped me from interrupting.) "His lips were moving, and I realized what he was saying was, 'And then she licks her palm.' You're not like that, Eric. You're more self-contained. And besides, we like each other, right?"

"We do," I said. "We really do," but it sounded tepid.

"I've definitely kissed less than half your cabin, by the way. I've been counting in my head and there's only four."

"Including Doron?"

"Okay, five. But you're no slouch either. How about that bellybutton shot with Cheryl?"

"That doesn't count. It was part of the bar mitzvah ceremony."

"Does this count?" she asked, bringing my hand up to her breast.

"It counts," I said, forming my fingers into a cup.

"And Trina!" she added, suddenly uproarious. "Admit it, Eric. You had socks with Trina." I felt my face reddening in the dark as the triplets approached.

"Do you and your sister need any help?" the instigator smirked.

"Nice outfits" I shot back. "Do you always dress alike?"

"Shorts and t-shirt don't cut it at the Chicago Board of Trade," he said.

"You're stockbrokers?" Tammy asked.

"Captains of industry," said the ringleader.

"Actually," confessed the coward, "my dad got us all summer internships."

A bright flash drew all of our glances to the Second Story window. At the center of a small crowd of faces, Oliver was grinning maniacally, pointing the orange pistol at the sky as sparks streaked across the night.

*RAT FUCK!* they screamed.

"What did they say?" asked the coward. "What was that?"

"We've got to shout something back," I explained. "'Chicken shit,' on the count of three. Ready? One... two...three!"

*CHICKEN SHIT!*

There was smoke in our eyes from the lingering sizzle and fizzle, and at first it was hard to see what the reaction was up in the Second Story, but then: *DONKEY DICK!*

The triplets were willing members of our team now, and a sandy blonde couple dressed in formalwear joined forces with us. We briefly consulted before hollering: *CRISPY CUNT!!!*

A police car pulled up, cherry top flashing, but it wasn't the Chicago Police Department. Three doors opened, and Chris Hanekamp, Vicki Faber, and Franklin Strauss emerged.

"What the goddamn hell," Faber howled, "have you done to my car?"

# DEUTERONOMY

# PART I

"I was supposed to be in Israel this summer."

"Yeah? But instead you decided to scream obscenities in the middle of the street?"

"You had to be there."

"Eric, I *was* there."

"I mean it made sense at the time."

It had taken twenty minutes to sort the crowd at Ohio and St. Clair. Oliver had brought two of his new friends down, a bald poet with enormous black eyeglasses and a high school science teacher with a handlebar mustache. (The poet called our Rat Fuck a work of genius.) They had greeted Strauss warmly. Tammy had realized that the ringleader's dad was her mom's oncologist. This coincidence had augured an intense bond between them that had made me feel obsolete.

Hanekamp had insisted on driving Oliver and Tammy back to camp. Faber had offered to take Strauss home, but then they had realized they couldn't abandon me, and another arrangement had been decided upon. Faber had climbed into the police car heading back to camp, which, it came to me later, probably meant she was sleeping with the detective—or wanted to. That had left the Jaguar, Strauss, and me.

"My wife and I went to Israel when she was pregnant with Rochelle," Strauss said. He was driving west on Grand Avenue, three fingertips on the bottom of the steering wheel, seemingly searching for an address. "It was right after the Six-Day War, and we belonged to one of the first groups to be admitted to see the Western Wall."

"That must have been amazing," I said. We were getting to the end of brightly lit downtown and into shadowy neighborhoods that made me want to lock my door.

"You would think so," he agreed. "But Jerusalem was burning hot. They were setting records. Even the Bedouins were keeling over. Luckily, we were staying in the only hotel in the city that actually had air conditioning that worked. This old priest on our tour decided he was the Messiah, and they took him away in an ambulance."

"What was the Wall like?"

"Mobbed. We had to shove our way through this crowd of bearded men bowing fervently in black suits. The stench nearly killed me, and when I finally made it to the front, it was like, 'Oh, that's it?' I felt nothing, just like Diana Morales."

"Diana who?"

"That girl in *A Chorus Line* who fails to feel like a melting ice cream cone. But I felt ashamed to feel nothing, so I acted like I was so moved and transformed, you know? But everybody could see right through me. Especially Peggy, who's earned a doctorate in seeing through me. She just stayed behind in the hotel room, ordering room service and watching *Peyton Place*. Here it is, our first stop."

He parallel parked with astonishing ease. Our first stop was the penthouse of a complex recently built around a kidney-shaped pool. The elevator doors opened upon a symphony of beige. The sectional, coffee table, and rug all more or less matched the window treatments, which were down, and the wallpaper, which had a subtle texture that could only be described as beige.

"Whose apartment is this, again?" I asked.

"I am the majority owner of an LLC that holds the mortgage."

"But nobody lives here?"

"Nobody lives in any of them, but sometimes people stay there for a period of days or weeks, just enough so they can't be declared vacant."

I tried to conceal my bafflement and surveyed the place in search of some sign of life. The clock on the microwave oven flashed 12:00. There was nothing in the refrigerator but French's Classic Mustard and a wheel of Pecorino-Romano. Beside the VCR: a stack of movies with titles like *Fraternity of Brawn* and *Marines on Leave*.

"Did we think Rochelle would actually be here?" I asked, searching in vain for a bar of soap.

"It occurred to me," he answered. "But it appears not to be the case."

"So should we go?"

"Let's."

✡

Back in the Jaguar, Strauss pressed a button on the dashboard, and a square drawer slid out. The car had a compact disc player as well one for cassette tapes. I had never handled a CD before, and when he asked me to retrieve one from the compartment between the seats, I had considerable trouble extricating Dave Grusin and Lee Ritenour's *Harlequin* from the plastic teeth around the hub of the jewel case.

"It was a hell of scene at camp," Strauss said. "Handle it by the edges. The oil from your fingerprints can distort the lasers." This jazz—I guess you would call it that—sounded precise and polished, the opposite of everything in Oliver's tape collection. It suited Strauss's black satin shirt and diamond pinky ring, his blow-dried tresses and marble cheekbones.

We weren't on a romantic adventure anymore. This was Strauss's odyssey through the corrupt heart of America. Accompanied by a sidekick who served little purpose other than comic relief, the tormented protagonist risked everything for something more than domestic bless, perhaps existential redemption. The air in the Jaguar had dropped by a few degrees, but my thighs still stuck to the leather interior. "What happened?" I asked.

"Very funny." The car hit a pothole, and the jazz stuttered and restarted. "First you play them the scariest-ever radio broadcast before bedtime, and then people start vanishing. These are children with active imaginations."

Smooth jazz stylings oiling our eardrums, we headed west into Oak Park. Strauss steered around a busy construction site and pulled over to study a map.

"Is there a key chain under the CD's?" I said there was. "We're going to check out a few more properties, and hopefully Peggy and Rochelle will be inside one of them. And Crockett, too." For the moment I couldn't place the name. "We adopted a Great Dane puppy in the spring. Peggy didn't like being alone so much. The breeder has a wall of international awards. That goddamn thing already weighs more than me."

"So Rabbi Mick's pretty mad?" I asked.

"You could say that. The next time your camper throws up in a trash receptacle, you might want to rinse it out instead of leaving it outside the cabin door. Not that there's going to be a next time."

"No, I guess not."

"At about 9:30 p.m., Rabbi Michael ('Mick') Harris, camp director of Paley Lithwick Strauss, stepped into the Rubbermaid full of vomit and proceeded to struggle for upwards of ten minutes to pull his boot out."

"In other words, yes, he's mad," I whimpered.

And then simultaneously we both added: "Hopping mad."

The next place was just as empty but more opulent. Pseudo-Impressionist art hung in gilded frames, and a long table set with china and silver, as though a banquet might materialize at any moment. Strauss held a crystal decanter up to the moonlight, inspecting for residue of an earlier bacchanal.

"Nice place," I said. "How much would it sell for?"

"Ninety-five, ninety-eight, somewhere in there," he answered. "Are you in the market?"

I cleared my throat. "*A commodity appears at first sight an extremely obvious, trivial thing. But its analysis brings out that it is a very strange thing, abounding in metaphysical subtleties and theological niceties.*"

"And that's supposed to mean something?"

"It's Karl Marx."

"Never heard of him. Is he in real estate, too?"

"How many apartments do you own all together?"

"Eighteen properties, not counting the one I keep for myself on Lake Shore Drive."

"Tammy Berk said you're in private equity."

"Real estate has become an accidental pastime. Never passing up a bargain is my curse."

"And ninety-five thousand dollars is a bargain for an apartment?"

"No, Eric. *Sixty-one* thousand was a bargain for *this* apartment."

Around midnight we merged onto the Tri-State Tollway and then turned off for our third stop, a recently built mansion in Naperville. The lawn was flawless, the crickets cacophonous. Strauss knocked, waited, and used the key. The power had been cut, so he went to the trunk to fetch his flashlight, which happened to be the same model that Andrew used to detect the presence of semen on pizza.

The house appeared to have been decorated by a professional under the influence of *Dallas*—call it pasteboard cowboy with a sprinkling of gold dust—but there was no sign that anyone had ever occupied it. For some reason, the dust particles swirling in Strauss's beam of light strongly suggested to me that we might come across Rochelle's body in one of these rooms. Her naked, lifeless body, to be precise. Wrenched into an unnatural shape and marinating in a pool of blood. This despite ample evidence that she was safe and sound with her mom and dog.

I dug into my pocket for the Milk Duds, something to clear my mouth of its bitter taste, and in my fumbling, the condom that Doron had given me fell out. Strauss shined his light on the floor and said nothing as I stuffed it back in my shorts.

# PART II

Strauss asked what my father did. It was the question I dreaded second most, after "Are you a virgin?" I tried to explain about parking garages and Dallas, making even less sense with my words than I did in my mind.

"Does he own the parking garages? Does he build them?"

"No, he's more of a go-between between the builder and the owner, I guess."

"Your mother and father are heading for divorce court," Strauss said. "That's what it sounds like to me."

"Nobody has used that word so far."

"Are they calling it a 'trial separation'?"

"He just says he has a lot going on in Dallas."

"We have a wide variety of parking garages right here in Chicagoland," Strauss said. "No offense." We crossed over into Kendall County, and I wondered whether this night would ever end and then whether I'd ever see my steamer trunk again and all my summer stuff. Owing to my poor sense of direction, I imagined we weren't too far from southern Wisconsin. I could feel its rural attraction and almost detect the smell of campfire in the night air.

A geometrically perfect structure, blindingly illuminated, lay ahead of us. It was like someone had sliced two stories off a high-rise office building, hauled it away and planted it in the prairie. We parked at the foot of a winding, freshly tarred driveway. A squadron of mosquitoes found us immediately, and our hands flapped madly as we approached the door.

"There are worse things than divorce," Strauss said. I didn't answer. "Think of all the horrible, debilitating diseases you could have had. Or your mother or father."

"I have an older brother, too," I said.

"Think of the guilt you'd feel if you backed over a toddler. That kind of thing would haunt you to your grave. Going to prison, you'd never recover from that, given what I've seen about prisons on *60 Minutes*. You have a good head on your shoulders. You're a good listener—at least you seem to be listening." I nodded vigorously. "In the long run, listening skills are more important, better for you, than whether your parents stay together or the girls in college let you stick your finger in them."

"I'd hate to miss out on that," I said. "Because of listening."

"Maybe you can have it all, Eric. Not my daughter, but everything else. Don't let anyone tell you you can't."

Suddenly, a loud, wet snarling made us both gasp. "Crockett!" Strauss said, recovering. "It's me, boy." This reassurance did not placate the animal. The door swung open, and a woman stood there, braced against the frame as the dog barked and dribbled, straining against the collar in the her grip.

"Get in, quick, but leave those bugs outside." The woman had black hair like Rochelle's, but stringy, and she wore an oversize bathrobe with a necktie knotted around her waist. She sent me to the fridge for a couple of cubes of raw steak. Crockett took one cube each from Strauss and me and curled up under the all-glass dining room table.

"There," she said. "Now he thinks you belong to the pack."

"I'm the leader of the pack, Peggy," grinned Strauss. "Remember when you fell for me?"

She poured something viscous and golden-brown into two heavy tumblers. Every wall of the house was made of thick plate glass. It felt like we were floating in a vast dark landscape.

Or we were science-fair subjects arranged in a neglected terrarium.

No, it felt like we were being projected onto an enormous drive-in screen. "This place must be amazing during a rainstorm," I said.

"Who's the weatherman?" she asked Strauss.

"My name is Eric Weintraub," I said. "And I'm one of Rochelle's counselors at camp."

"I found him in downtown Chicago," explained Strauss, "shouting about crispy cunts, so I brought him along for company."

"Good, we could use a ladies' man."

"Where is Rochelle?" I asked. "Did she come here with you?"

"We're on the lam," Peggy Strauss said, gesturing around her ironically. "My daughter and I and that beast you fed. As opposed to the beast I married and the hundred-dollar-an-hour law firm he's going to hire when I try to divorce him, which ultimately is what we're on the lam from." She was every bit as gorgeous as her daughter. Unkempt, in a Ritz bathrobe, worn out from worry and the road, she radiated serenity—and glamour—well beyond her daughter's range.

"People were concerned," Strauss said. "Not just the weatherman."

"It's not kidnapping if it's your own daughter," she said.

"Nobody said anything about kidnapping, Peggy. And nobody's getting a divorce. Except for Eric's mother and father, I'm afraid."

"So Rochelle is here?" I asked again. "Like, in this house?" Peggy had driven up to camp in the dead of night and retrieved Rochelle, taking precaution to disguise her, not to protect the girl but as leverage in an unfiled divorce case. What was the line in the Bauhaus song, about *Hot heads under silent wigs*? Would I be called upon to testify? Whose side was I on?

"Feel free to search the place," she said. "That is, if you have a warrant."

Just then Rochelle entered, wearing nothing but black underpants, but, owing to an enormous set of headphones, unaware of our presence.

"Mom, my ostrich slaughter is killing me. Do we have any Tylenol?"

When it registered to her that Peggy wasn't the only other person in the house, she turned on her father with astonishing fury.

"What the fuck are you even doing here, you cheater, you fucking AIDS case?" She swung the heels of her hands at his face as he hung his head but did not shield himself. The dog came out from under the table and snarled at the melee.

"Are you through?" he said.

"From now on I'm going by 'Rochelle La Vraie'," she yelled. "I always hated the name Strauss."

"Me too," added Peggy. "But put on some clothes. We have company."

Rochelle crossed her arms but did not budge. Strauss reached out to stroke Crockett but appeared not to be part of the pack anymore. The animal lunged at him, straining against Peggy's grip.

"Fuck this dog!"

"You fuck it, you're the pervert here," Rochelle sneered.

"How about your friend fucks it," Strauss answered. "He brought protection."

"He's not my friend, he's my counselor, and his name is Eric. Or didn't you bother asking on the drive down?"

Many years later, the meaning of "ostrich slaughter" came to me. She was referring to her Osgood-Schlatter disease, a common cause of knee pain in adolescents.

Peggy finished her drink and reached for Strauss's, which he hadn't touched. "Did he take you on the full tour of his underground railroad for the cabaret set?" she asked me.

"We hit the highlights," I said.

Rochelle finally went in the back for clothes while Strauss fed the dog cube after bloody cube of raw meat, trying to win back his affection. The silk shirt, which I'd thought was black the whole time, turned out to be the deepest possible blue. It was still tucked neatly into immaculate white jeans, and he wore suede moccasins on his bare feet.

"Does the VHS work in this place?" he asked.

"I saved some bacon grease," Peggy added. It was a non sequitur to me, but the others caught on. Rochelle returned with a green, pink, and purple Ton Sur Ton sweatshirt and a tin of Tiger Balm for her knee.

✡

The cabinet of movies was heavy on the golden age of melodrama. We went with *Whatever Happened to Baby Jane?* costarring Bette Davis as a former Vaudeville star and Joan Crawford as her crippled sister. We wisecracked all over the dialogue, alternately impersonating the characters and warning them not to believe each other. The bacon-grease popcorn was both as delicious and as disgusting as it sounds. Toward the end, when the sisters flee to the beach, Rochelle rested her head on my shoulder and Tiger Balm-infused air filled my sinuses. When the movie was over, Strauss offered me a ride back to camp.

"Just Morton Grove, thanks," I said. "They were kicking me out anyway, because of my terrorist sympathies."

"It would take just one phone call," Strauss said. "And none of this ever happened. Mick is my bitch, now that they put my name on the camp."

"Not necessary."

"Okay," he shrugged. "But what's the point of being generous if you

**119**

can't demand special treatment?"

"They inscribe your name in the Book of Life," I answered.

"Better be in huge fucking type," he said. "Page one."

✡

I crossed out line after line from the lyrics to the Rochelle song I was trying to write between camp and college. Entire verses went into the trash. The whole fox-mermaid scheme fell apart when I introduced the glass house, which, for one thing, didn't make sense for a mermaid, and for another, had already been used by Billy Joel. In one version, an angelfish pursued a sea-horse around a dirty aquarium, but that, too, was torn out of the notebook and ripped into little pieces. On the other hand, the chord progression never failed to capture the way I felt, and I would play it over and over again, first stately and then torrid, waiting for the right words to strike, but all that survived was the Rhymin' Simon-worthy couplet

*She said the bedroom door's unlocked.*
*But no one answers when you knock.*

And that sufficed for me, for the time being. As Rabbi Nachman of Breslov wrote, "One must be careful not to talk more than necessary. Just as much as is necessary for the creation of the world, no more.

# ACKNOWLEDGMENTS

Constant eternal gratitude to
Jennie Guilfoyle, Jasper Swartz & Rebecca Guilfoyle

Heartfelt appreciation to Tony Ross

Special thanks to Alan Berlin, Myles Feingold-Black, Kevin Flagg,
Elise Gould, Anna Kunz, Sam Lieberman, Darcy Lockman,
Devin McIntyre, Mitch Silver, Michelle Silverman, Steve Silverman,
Laurel Swartz, Michael Swartz, Robert Swartz

PLAYLIST

*The author asserts Fair Use for song lyrics and other texts
quoted in this novel, from the following works:*

Paul Simon, "The Boy in the Bubble"
Words and Music by Paul Simon and Forere Mothoeloa © 1986

The Mystic Knights of Oingo Boingo, "Nuclear Babies."
© Danny and Richard Elfman. See
https://www.youtube.com/watch?v=h0W9OCjxkD8

Simple Minds, "Promised You a Miracle."
Written by Charles Burchill / Derek Forbes
/ James Kerr / Michael Joseph Mac Neil
© Sony/ATV Music Publishing LLC, BMG Rights Management

Ultravox, "When You Walk through Me."
Written by Dennis Leigh / Robin Simon / William Currie
© Universal Music Publishing Group

Robert Pirsig, *Zen and the Art of Motorcycle Maintenance: An Inquiry into Values.*
William Morrow & Co., 1974

Squeeze, "Take Me I'm Yours."
Written by Christopher Henry Difford / Glenn Martin Tilbrook.
© Universal Music Publishing Group

Bob Dylan, "Tomorrow Is a Long Time."
© 1963 by Warner Bros. Inc.; renewed 1991 by Special Rider Music

Scott MacLeod, "A Dangerous Occupation,"
*The New York Review of Books,* August 16, 1984

James Taylor and Carly Simon, "Mockingbird."
Written by Charlie Foxx / Inez Foxx © Sony/ATV Music Publishing LLC

## ABOUT THE AUTHOR

Mark Swartz is the author of the novels
*Instant Karma* (City Lights, 2002) and *H2O* (Soft Skull, 2006).

He lives with his family in Takoma Park, Maryland,
and helps organizations tell their stories.

www.swartzmark.com

Made in the USA
Middletown, DE
26 November 2023

43596205R00076